More praise for

FLIPPED

"We flipped over this fantastic book, its gutsy girl Juli and its wise, wonderful ending."

—*The Chicago Tribune*

"Delightful! Delicious! And totally teen."

—*BookPage*

★ "With a charismatic leading lady kids will flip over, a compelling dynamic between the two narrators and a resonant ending, this novel is a great deal larger than the sum of its parts."

—*Publishers Weekly*, Starred

"A wonderful, light-hearted novel."

—*Library Talk*

"This is a wry character study, a romance with substance and subtlety."

—*Booklist*

"A highly agreeable romantic comedy."

—*Kirkus Reviews*

WENDELIN VAN DRAANEN

FLIPPED

SCHOLASTIC INC.
New York   Toronto   London   Auckland   Sydney
Mexico City   New Delhi   Hong Kong   Buenos Aires

ISBN 0-439-64998-6

12 11 10 9 8 7 6 5 4 3 2   4 5 6 7 8 9/0

Printed in the U.S.A.   40

First Scholastic printing, January 2004

Dedicated with infinite love to

Colton and Connor,

who make me feel like so much more than the sum of my parts.

Special thanks to . . .

my husband, Mark Parsons,

who helps me feel the magic,

and

my excellent editor, Nancy Siscoe,

for her care and insight

(and for making me stick to a reduced-filler diet).

Also, eternal gratitude to

Tad Callahan and Patricia Gabel,

who were on the ball when we needed it most.

Finally, thanks to Jeanne Madrid and the staff at Casa De Vida—

may you keep the spirit.

CONTENTS

Diving Under 1

Flipped 11

Buddy, Beware! 20

The Sycamore Tree 32

Brawk-Brawk-Brawk! 44

The Eggs 63

Get a Grip, Man 81

The Yard 100

Looming Large and Smelly 117

The Visit 129

The Serious Willies 145

The Dinner 159

Flipped 170

The Basket Boys 189

Diving Under

All I've ever wanted is for Juli Baker to leave me alone. For her to back off—you know, just give me some *space*.

It all started the summer before second grade when our moving van pulled into her neighborhood. And since we're now about done with the *eighth* grade, that, my friend, makes more than half a decade of strategic avoidance and social discomfort.

She didn't just barge into my life. She barged and shoved and wedged her way into my life. Did we invite her to get into our moving van and start climbing all over boxes? No! But that's exactly what she did, taking over and showing off like only Juli Baker can.

My dad tried to stop her. "Hey!" he says as she's catapulting herself on board. "What are you doing? You're getting mud everywhere!" So true, too. Her shoes were, like, caked with the stuff.

She didn't hop out, though. Instead, she planted her rear end on the floor and started pushing a big box with her feet. "Don't you want some help?" She glanced my way. "It sure looks like you *need* it."

I didn't like the implication. And even though my dad had been tossing me the same sort of look all week, I could tell—he didn't like this girl either. "Hey! Don't do that," he warned her. "There are some really valuable things in that box."

"Oh. Well, how about this one?" She scoots over to a box labeled LENOX and looks my way again. "We should push it together!"

"No, no, no!" my dad says, then pulls her up by the arm. "Why don't you run along home? Your mother's probably wondering where you are."

This was the beginning of my soon-to-become-acute awareness that the girl cannot take a hint. Of any kind. Does she zip on home like a kid should when they've been invited to leave? No. She says, "Oh, my mom knows where I am. She said it was fine." Then she points across the street and says, "We just live right over there."

My father looks to where she's pointing and mutters, "Oh boy." Then he looks at me and winks as he says, "Bryce, isn't it time for you to go inside and help your mother?"

I knew right off that this was a ditch play. And I didn't think about it until later, but ditch wasn't a play I'd run with my dad before. Face it, pulling a ditch is not something discussed with dads. It's like, against parental law to tell your kid it's okay to ditch someone, no matter how annoying or *muddy* they might be.

But there he was, putting the play in motion, and man, he didn't have to wink twice. I smiled and said, "Sure thing!" then jumped off the liftgate and headed for my new front door.

I heard her coming after me but I couldn't believe it. Maybe it just sounded like she was chasing me; maybe she was really going the other way. But before I got up the nerve to look, she blasted right past me, grabbing my arm and yanking me along.

This was too much. I planted myself and was about to tell her to get lost when the weirdest thing happened. I was making this big windmill motion to break away from her, but somehow on the downswing my hand wound up tangling into hers. I couldn't believe it. There I was, holding the mud monkey's hand!

I tried to shake her off, but she just clamped on tight and yanked me along, saying, "C'mon!"

My mom came out of the house and immediately got the world's sappiest look on her face. "Well, hello," she says to Juli.

"Hi!"

I'm still trying to pull free, but the girl's got me in a death grip. My mom's grinning, looking at our hands and my fiery red face. "And what's your name, honey?"

"Julianna Baker. I live right over there," she says, pointing with her unoccupied hand.

"Well, I see you've met my son," she says, still grinning away.

"Uh-huh!"

Finally I break free and do the only manly thing available when you're seven years old—I dive behind my mother.

Mom puts her arm around me and says, "Bryce, honey, why don't you show Julianna around the house?"

I flash her help and warning signals with every part of my body, but she's not receiving. Then *she* shakes *me* off and says, "Go on."

3

Juli would've tramped right in if my mother hadn't noticed her shoes and told her to take them off. And after those were off, my mom told her that her dirty socks had to go, too. Juli wasn't embarrassed. Not a bit. She just peeled them off and left them in a crusty heap on our porch.

I didn't exactly give her a tour. I locked myself in the bathroom instead. And after about ten minutes of yelling back at her that no, I wasn't coming out anytime soon, things got quiet out in the hall. Another ten minutes went by before I got the nerve to peek out the door.

No Juli.

I snuck out and looked around, and yes! She was gone.

Not a very sophisticated ditch, but hey, I was only seven.

My troubles were far from over, though. Every day she came back, over and over again. "Can Bryce play?" I could hear her asking from my hiding place behind the couch. "Is he ready yet?" One time she even cut across the yard and looked through my window. I spotted her in the nick of time and dove under my bed, but man, that right there tells you something about Juli Baker. She's got no concept of personal space. No respect for privacy. The world is her playground, and watch out below— Juli's on the slide!

Lucky for me, my dad was willing to run block. And he did it over and over again. He told her I was busy or sleeping or just plain gone. He was a lifesaver.

My sister, on the other hand, tried to sabotage me any chance she got. Lynetta's like that. She's four years older than me, and buddy, I've learned from watching her how not to run your life. She's got ANTAGONIZE written all over her. Just look at her—not cross-eyed or with your tongue sticking out or anything—just *look* at her and you've started an argument.

I used to knock-down-drag-out with her, but it's just not worth it. Girls don't fight fair. They pull your hair and gouge you and pinch you; then they run off gasping to mommy when you try and defend yourself with a fist. Then you get locked into time-out, and for what? No, my friend, the secret is, don't snap at the bait. Let it dangle. Swim around it. Laugh it off. After a while they'll give up and try to lure someone else.

At least that's the way it is with Lynetta. And the bonus of having her as a pain-in-the-rear sister was figuring out that this method works on everyone. Teachers, jerks at school, even Mom and Dad. Seriously. There's no winning arguments with your parents, so why get all pumped up over them? It is way better to dive down and get out of the way than it is to get clobbered by some parental tidal wave.

The funny thing is, Lynetta's still clueless when it comes to dealing with Mom and Dad. She goes straight into thrash mode and is too busy drowning in the argument to take a deep breath and dive for calmer water.

And she thinks *I'm* stupid.

Anyway, true to form, Lynetta tried to bait me with Juli those first few days. She even snuck her past Dad once and marched her all around the house, hunting me down. I wedged myself up on the top shelf of my closet, and lucky for me, neither of them looked up. A

5

few minutes later I heard Dad yell at Juli to get off the antique furniture, and once again, she got booted.

I don't think I went outside that whole first week. I helped unpack stuff and watched TV and just kind of hung around while my mom and dad arranged and rearranged the furniture, debating whether Empire settees and French Rococo tables should even be put in the same room.

So believe me, I was dying to go outside. But every time I checked through the window, I could see Juli showing off in her yard. She'd be heading a soccer ball or doing high kicks with it or dribbling it up and down their driveway. And when she wasn't busy showing off, she'd just sit on the curb with the ball between her feet, staring at our house.

My mom didn't understand why it was so awful that "that cute little girl" had held my hand. She thought I should make *friends* with her. "I thought you liked soccer, honey. Why don't you go out there and kick the ball around?"

Because *I* didn't want to be kicked around, that's why. And although I couldn't say it like that at the time, I still had enough sense at age seven and a half to know that Juli Baker was dangerous.

Unavoidably dangerous, as it turns out. The minute I walked into Mrs. Yelson's second-grade classroom, I was dead meat. "Bryce!" Juli squeals. "You're *here*." Then she charges across the room and tackles me.

Mrs. Yelson tried to explain this attack away as a "welcome hug," but man, that was no hug. That was a front-line, take-'em-down tackle. And even though I shook her off, it was too late. I was branded for life. Everyone jeered, "Where's your *girl*friend, Bryce?" "Are you *married* yet, Bryce?" And then when she chased me around at recess and tried to lay *kisses* on me, the whole school started singing, "Bryce and Juli sitting in a tree, K-I-S-S-I-N-G . . ."

My first year in town was a disaster.

Third grade wasn't much better. She was still hot on my trail every time I turned around. Same with fourth. But then in fifth grade I took action.

It started out slow—one of those Nah-that's-not-right ideas you get and forget. But the more I played with the idea, the more I thought, What better way to ward Juli off? What better way to say to her, "Juli, you are *not* my type"?

And so, my friend, I hatched the plan.

I asked Shelly Stalls out.

To fully appreciate the brilliance of this, you have to understand that Juli *hates* Shelly Stalls. She always has, though it beats me why. Shelly's nice and she's friendly and she's got a lot of hair. What's not to like? But Juli hated her, and I was going to make this little gem of knowledge the solution to my problem.

What I was thinking was that Shelly would eat lunch at our table and maybe walk around a little with me. That way, anytime Juli was around, all I'd have to do was hang a little closer to Shelly and things would just naturally take care of themselves. What *happened,* though, is that Shelly took things way too seriously. She went around telling everybody—including Juli—that we were in love.

In no time Juli and Shelly got into some kind of

7

catfight, and while Shelly was recovering from that, my supposed friend Garrett—who had been totally behind this plan—told her what I was up to. He's always denied it, but I've since learned that his code of honor is easily corrupted by weepy females.

That afternoon the principal tried cross-examining me, but I wouldn't cop to anything. I just kept telling her that I was sorry and that I really didn't understand what had happened. Finally she let me go.

Shelly cried for days and followed me around school sniffling and making me feel like a real jerk, which was even worse than having Juli as a shadow.

Everything blew over at the one-week mark, though, when Shelly officially dumped me and started going out with Kyle Larsen. Then Juli started up with the goo-goo eyes again, and I was back to square one.

Now, in sixth grade things changed, though whether they improved is hard to say. I don't remember Juli actually chasing me in the sixth grade. But I do remember her sniffing me.

Yes, my friend, I said sniffing.

And you can blame that on our teacher, Mr. Mertins. He stuck Juli to me like glue. Mr. Mertins has got some kind of doctorate in seating arrangements or something, because he analyzed and scrutinized and practically baptized the seats we had to sit in. And of course he decided to seat Juli right next to me.

Juli Baker is the kind of annoying person who makes a point of letting you know she's smart. Her hand is the first one up; her answers are usually complete dissertations; her projects are always turned in early and used as weapons against the rest of the class. Teachers always have to hold her project up and say, "*This* is what I'm looking for, class. This is an example of A-plus work." Add all the extra credit she does to an already perfect score, and I swear she's never gotten less than 120 percent in any subject.

But after Mr. Mertins stuck Juli right next to me, her annoying knowledge of all subjects far and wide came in handy. See, suddenly Juli's perfect answers, written in perfect cursive, were right across the aisle, just an eye-shot away. You wouldn't believe the number of answers I snagged from her. I started getting A's and B's on everything! It was great!

But then Mr. Mertins pulled the shift. He had some new idea for "optimizing positional latitude and longitude," and when the dust finally settled, I was sitting right in front of Juli Baker.

This is where the sniffing comes in. That maniac started leaning forward and *sniffing* my hair. She'd edge her nose practically up to my scalp and *sniff-sniff-sniff*.

I tried elbowing and back-kicking. I tried scooting my chair way forward or putting my backpack between me and the seat. Nothing helped. She'd just scoot up, too, or lean over a little farther and *sniff-sniff-sniff*.

I finally asked Mr. Mertins to move me, but he wouldn't do it. Something about not wanting to disturb the delicate balance of educational energies.

Whatever. I was stuck with her sniffing. And since I couldn't see her perfectly penned answers anymore, my grades took a dive. Especially in spelling.

Then one time, during a test, Juli's in the middle of

9

sniffing my hair when she notices that I've blown a spelling word. A lot of words. Suddenly the sniffing stops and the whispering starts. At first I couldn't believe it. Juli Baker cheating? But sure enough, she was spelling words for me, right in my ear.

Juli'd always been sly about sniffing, which really bugged me because no one ever noticed her doing it, but she was just as sly about giving me answers, which was okay by me. The bad thing about it was that I started counting on her spelling in my ear. I mean, why study when you don't have to, right? But after a while, taking all those answers made me feel sort of indebted to her. How can you tell someone to bug off or quit sniffing you when you owe them? It's, you know, wrong.

So I spent the sixth grade somewhere between uncomfortable and unhappy, but I kept thinking that next year, *next* year, things would be different. We'd be in junior high—a big school—in different classes. It would be a world with too many people to worry about ever seeing Juli Baker again.

It was finally, *finally* going to be over.

Flipped

The first day I met Bryce Loski, I flipped. Honestly, one look at him and I became a lunatic. It's his eyes. Something in his eyes. They're blue, and framed in the blackness of his lashes, they're dazzling. Absolutely breathtaking.

It's been over six years now, and I learned long ago to hide my feelings, but oh, those first days. Those first years! I thought I would die for wanting to be with him.

Two days before the second grade is when it started, although the anticipation began weeks before—ever since my mother had told me that there was a family with a boy my age moving into the new house right across the street.

Soccer camp had ended, and I'd been so bored because there was nobody, absolutely nobody, in the neighborhood to play with. Oh, there were kids, but every one of them was older. That was dandy for my brothers, but what it left *me* was home alone.

My mother was there, but she had better things to do than kick a soccer ball around. So she said, anyway. At the time I didn't think there was anything better than kicking a soccer ball around, especially not the likes of laundry or dishes or vacuuming, but my mother didn't agree. And the danger of being home alone with her was that she'd recruit me to help her wash or dust or vacuum, and she wouldn't tolerate the dribbling of a soccer ball around the house as I moved from chore to chore.

To play it safe, I waited outside for weeks, just in case the new neighbors moved in early. Literally, it was *weeks*. I entertained myself by playing soccer with our dog, Champ. Mostly he'd just block because a dog can't exactly kick and score, but once in a while he'd dribble with his nose. The scent of a ball must overwhelm a dog, though, because Champ would eventually try to chomp it, then lose the ball to me.

When the Loskis' moving van finally arrived, everyone in my family was happy. "Little Julianna" was finally going to have a playmate.

My mother, being the truly sensible adult that she is, made me wait more than an *hour* before going over to meet him. "Give them a chance to stretch their legs, Julianna," she said. "They'll want some time to adjust." She wouldn't even let me watch from the yard. "I know you, sweetheart. Somehow that ball will wind up in their yard and you'll just *have* to go retrieve it."

So I watched from the window, and every few minutes I'd ask, "Now?" and she'd say, "Give them a little while longer, would you?"

Then the phone rang. And the minute I was sure she was good and preoccupied, I tugged on her sleeve and asked, "Now?"

She nodded and whispered, "Okay, but take it easy! I'll be over there in a minute."

I was too excited not to charge across the street, but I did try very hard to be civilized once I got to the moving van. I stood outside looking in for a record-breaking length of time, which was hard because there he was! About halfway back! My new sure-to-be best friend, Bryce Loski.

Bryce wasn't really doing much of anything. He was more hanging back, watching his father move boxes onto the lift-gate. I remember feeling sorry for Mr. Loski because he looked worn out, moving boxes all by himself. I also remember that he and Bryce were wearing matching turquoise polo shirts, which I thought was really cute. Really *nice*.

When I couldn't stand it any longer, I called, "Hi!" into the van, which made Bryce jump, and then quick as a cricket, he started pushing a box like he'd been working all along.

I could tell from the way Bryce was acting so guilty that he was supposed to be moving boxes, but he was sick of it. He'd probably been moving things for days! It was easy to see that he needed a rest. He needed some juice! Something.

It was also easy to see that Mr. Loski wasn't about to let him quit. He was going to keep on moving boxes around until he collapsed, and by then Bryce might be dead. Dead before he'd had the chance to move in!

The tragedy of it catapulted me into the moving van. I had to help! I had to save him!

When I got to his side to help him shove a box forward, the poor boy was so exhausted that he just moved aside and let me take over. Mr. Loski didn't want me to help, but at least I saved Bryce. I'd been in the moving van all of three minutes when his dad sent him off to help his mother unpack things inside the house.

I chased Bryce up the walkway, and that's when every-thing changed. You see, I caught up to him and grabbed his

13

arm, trying to stop him so maybe we could play a little before he got trapped inside, and the next thing I know he's holding my hand, looking right into my eyes.

My heart stopped. It just stopped beating. And for the first time in my life, I had that feeling. You know, like the world is moving all around you, all beneath you, all *inside* you, and you're floating. Floating in midair. And the only thing keeping you from drifting away is the other person's eyes. They're connected to yours by some invisible physical force, and they hold you fast while the rest of the world swirls and twirls and falls completely away.

I almost got my first kiss that day. I'm sure of it. But then his mother came out the front door and he was so embarrassed that his cheeks turned completely red, and the next thing you know he's hiding in the bathroom.

I was waiting for him to come out when his sister, Lynetta, saw me in the hallway. She seemed big and mature to me, and since she wanted to know what was going on, I told her a little bit about it. I shouldn't have, though, because she wiggled the bathroom doorknob and started teasing Bryce something fierce. "Hey, baby brother!" she called through the door. "There's a hot chick out here waiting for you! Whatsa matter? Afraid she's got cooties?"

It was so embarrassing! I yanked on her arm and told her to stop it, but she wouldn't, so finally I just left.

I found my mother outside talking to Mrs. Loski. Mom had given her the beautiful lemon Bundt cake that was supposed to be our dessert that night. The powdered sugar looked soft and white, and the cake was still warm, sending sweet lemon smells into the air.

14

My mouth was watering just looking at it! But it was in Mrs. Loski's hands, and I knew there was no getting it back. All I could do was try to eat up the smells while I listened to the two of them discuss grocery stores and the weather forecast.

After that Mom and I went home. It was very strange. I hadn't gotten to play with Bryce at all. All I knew was that his eyes were a dizzying blue, that he had a sister who was not to be trusted, and that he'd almost kissed me.

I fell asleep that night thinking about the kiss that might have been. What did a kiss feel like, anyway? Somehow I knew it wouldn't be like the one I got from Mom or Dad at bedtime. The same species, maybe, but a radically different beast, to be sure. Like a wolf and a whippet—only science would put them on the same tree.

15

Looking back on the second grade, I like to think it was at least partly scientific curiosity that made me chase after that kiss, but to be honest, it was probably more those blue eyes. All through the second and third grades I couldn't seem to stop myself from following him, from sitting by him, from just wanting to be near him.

By the fourth grade I'd learned to control myself. The sight of him—the thought of him—still sent my heart humming, but my legs didn't actually chase after him anymore. I just watched and thought and dreamed.

Then in the fifth grade Shelly Stalls came into the picture. Shelly Stalls is a ninny. A whiny, gossipy, backstabbing ninny who says one thing to one person and the opposite to another. Now that we're in junior high, she's the undisputed diva of drama, but even back in elementary school she knew how to put on a performance. Especially when it came to P.E. I never once saw her run laps or do calisthenics. Instead, she would go into her "delicate" act, claiming her body would absolutely collapse from the strain if she ran or jumped or stretched.

It worked. Every year. She'd bring in some note and be sure to swoon a little for the teacher the first few days of the year, after which she'd be excused from anything that required muscles. She never even put up her own chair at the end of the day. The only muscles she exercised regularly were the ones around her mouth, and those she worked out nonstop. If there was an Olympic contest for talking, Shelly Stalls would sweep the event. Well, she'd at least win the gold and silver— one medal for each side of her mouth.

What bugged me about it was not the fact that she got out of P.E.—who'd want her on their team, anyway? What bugged me about it was that anyone who bothered to look would know that it wasn't asthma or weak ankles or her being "delicate" that was stopping her. It was her hair. She had mountains of it, twisted this way or that, clipped or beaded, braided or swirled. Her ponytails rivaled the ones on carousel horses. And on the days she let it all hang down, she'd sort of shimmy and cuddle inside it like it was a blanket, so that practically all you saw of her face was her nose. Good luck playing four-square with a blanket over your head.

My solution to Shelly Stalls was to ignore her, which worked just dandy until about halfway through the fifth grade when I saw her holding hands with Bryce.

My Bryce. The one who was still embarrassed over holding my hand two days before the second grade. The one who was still too shy to say much more than hello to me.

The one who was still walking around with my first kiss.

How could Shelly have wormed her hand into his? That pushy little princess had no business hanging on to him like that!

Bryce looked over his shoulder from time to time as they walked along, and he was looking at *me*. My first thought was that he was telling me he was sorry. Then it dawned on me—he needed my help. Absolutely, that's what it had to be! Shelly Stalls was too delicate to shake off, too swirly to be pushed away. She'd unravel and start sniffling and oh, how embarrassing that would be for him! No, this wasn't a job a boy could do gracefully. This was a job for a girl.

I didn't even bother checking around for other candidates—I had her off of him in two seconds flat. Bryce ran away the minute he was free, but not Shelly. Oh, no-no-no! She came at me, scratching and pulling and twisting anything she could get her hands on, telling me that Bryce was *hers* and there was no way she was letting him go.

How delicate.

I was hoping for herds of teachers to appear so they could see the real Shelly Stalls in action, but it was too late by the time anyone arrived on the scene. I had Fluffy in a headlock and her arm twisted back in a hammerlock, and no amount of her squawking or scratching was going to get me to *un*lock her until a teacher arrived.

In the end, Shelly went home early with a bad case of mussed-up hair, while I told my side of things to the principal. Mrs. Shultz is a sturdy lady who probably secretly appreciates the value of a swift kick well placed, and although she told me that it would be better if I let other people work out their own

17

dilemmas, she definitely understood about Shelly Stalls and her hair and told me she was glad I'd had the self-control to do nothing more than restrain her.

Shelly was back the next day with a head full of braids. And of course she got everybody whispering about me, but I just ignored them. The facts spoke for themselves. Bryce didn't go anywhere near her for the rest of the year.

That's not to say that Bryce held *my* hand after that, but he did start being a little friendlier to me. Especially in the sixth grade, after Mr. Mertins sat us right next to each other in the third row back.

Sitting next to Bryce was nice. *He* was nice. He'd say Hi, Juli to me every morning, and once in a while I'd catch him looking my way. He'd always blush and go back to his own work, and I couldn't help but smile. He was so shy. And so cute!

We talked to each other more, too. Especially after Mr. Mertins moved me behind him. Mr. Mertins had a detention policy about spelling, where if you missed more than seven out of twenty-five words, you had to spend lunch inside with him, writing your words over and over and over again.

The pressure of detention made Bryce panic. And even though it bothered my conscience, I'd lean in and whisper answers to him, hoping that maybe *I* could spend lunch with him instead. His hair smelled like watermelon, and his earlobes had fuzz. Soft, blond fuzz. And I wondered about that. How does a boy with such black hair wind up with blond ear fuzz? What's it doing there, anyway? I checked my own earlobes in the mirror but couldn't find much of anything on them, and I didn't spot any on other people's either.

JULIANNA

I thought about asking Mr. Mertins about earlobe fuzz when we were discussing evolution in science, but I didn't. Instead, I spent the year whispering spelling words, sniffing watermelon, and wondering if I was ever going to get my kiss.

Buddy, Beware!

Seventh grade brought changes, all right, but the biggest one didn't happen at school—it happened at home. Granddad Duncan came to live with us.

At first it was kind of weird because none of us really knew him. Except for Mom, of course. And even though she's spent the past year and a half trying to convince us he's a great guy, from what I can tell, the thing he likes to do best is stare out the front-room window. There's not much to see out there except the Bakers' front yard, but you can find him there day or night, sitting in the big easy chair they moved in with him, staring out the window.

Okay, so he also reads Tom Clancy novels and the newspapers and does crossword puzzles and tracks his stocks, but those things are all distractions. Given no one to justify it to, the man would stare out the window until he fell asleep. Not that there's anything wrong with that. It just seems so...boring.

Mom says he stares like that because he misses Grandma, but that's not something Granddad had ever discussed with me. As a matter of fact, he never discussed much of anything with me until a few months ago when he read about Juli in the newspaper.

Now, Juli Baker did not wind up on the front page of

the *Mayfield Times* for being an eighth-grade Einstein, like you might suspect. No, my friend, she got front-page coverage because she refused to climb out of a sycamore tree.

Not that I could tell a sycamore from a maple or a *birch* for that matter, but Juli, of course, knew what kind of tree it was and passed that knowledge along to every creature in her wake.

So this tree, this *sycamore* tree, was up the hill on a vacant lot on Collier Street, and it was massive. Massive and ugly. It was twisted and gnarled and bent, and I kept expecting the thing to blow over in the wind.

One day last year I'd finally had enough of her yakking about that stupid tree. I came right out and told her that it was not a magnificent sycamore, it was, in reality, the ugliest tree known to man. And you know what she said? She said I was visually challenged. Visually challenged! This from the girl who lives in a house that's the scourge of the neighborhood. They've got bushes growing over windows, weeds sticking out all over the place, and a barnyard's worth of animals running wild. I'm talking dogs, cats, chickens, even snakes. I swear to God, her brothers have a boa constrictor in their room. They dragged me in there when I was about ten and made me watch it eat a rat. A live, beady-eyed rat. They held that rodent up by its tail and *gulp,* the boa swallowed it whole. That snake gave me nightmares for a month.

Anyway, normally I wouldn't care about someone's yard, but the Bakers' mess bugged my dad big-time, and he channeled his frustration into *our* yard. He said it was

21

our neighborly duty to show them what a yard's supposed to look like. So while Mike and Matt are busy plumping up their boa, I'm having to mow and edge our yard, then sweep the walkways and *gutter*, which is going a little overboard, if you ask me.

And you'd think Juli's dad—who's a big, strong, brick-laying dude—would fix the place up, but no. According to my mom, he spends all his free time painting. His landscapes don't seem like anything special to me, but judging by his price tags, he thinks quite a lot of them. We see them every year at the Mayfield County Fair, and my parents always say the same thing: "The world would have more beauty in it if he'd fix up the yard instead."

22

Mom and Juli's mom do talk some. I think my mom feels sorry for Mrs. Baker—she says she married a dreamer, and because of that, one of the two of them will always be unhappy.

Whatever. Maybe Juli's aesthetic sensibilities have been permanently screwed up by her father and none of this is her fault, but Juli has always thought that that sycamore tree was God's gift to our little corner of the universe.

Back in the third and fourth grades she used to clown around with her brothers in the branches or peel big chunks of bark off so they could slide down the crook in its trunk. It seemed like they were playing in it whenever my mom took us somewhere in the car. Juli'd be swinging from the branches, ready to fall and break every bone in her body, while we were waiting at the stoplight, and my mom would shake her head and say, "Don't you ever climb that tree like that, do you hear me,

Bryce? I never want to see you doing that! You either, Lynetta. That is much too dangerous."

My sister would roll her eyes and say, "As *if*," while I'd slump beneath the window and pray for the light to change before Juli squealed my name for the world to hear.

I did try to climb it once in the fifth grade. It was the day after Juli had rescued my kite from its mutant toy-eating foliage. She climbed *miles* up to get my kite, and when she came down, she was actually very cool about it. She didn't hold my kite hostage and stick her lips out like I was afraid she might. She just handed it over and then backed away.

I was relieved, but I also felt like a weenie. When I'd seen where my kite was trapped, I was sure it was a goner. Not Juli. She scrambled up and got it down in no time. Man, it was embarrassing.

So I made a mental picture of how high she'd climbed, and the next day I set off to outdo her by at least two branches. I made it past the crook, up a few limbs, and then—just to see how I was doing—I looked down.

Mis-take! It felt like I was on top of the Empire State Building without a bungee. I tried looking up to where my kite had been, but it was hopeless. I was indeed a tree-climbing weenie.

Then junior high started and my dream of a Juli-free existence shattered. I had to take the bus, and you-know-who did, too. There were about eight kids altogether at our bus stop, which created a buffer zone, but it was no comfort zone. Juli always tried to stand beside me, or talk to me, or in some other way mortify me.

23

And then she started climbing. The girl is in the seventh grade, and she's climbing a tree—way, way up in a tree. And why does she do it? So she can yell down at us that the bus is five! four! three blocks away! Blow-by-blow traffic watch from a tree—what every kid in junior high feels like hearing first thing in the morning.

She tried to get me to come up there with her, too. "Bryce, come on! You won't believe the colors! It's absolutely magnificent! Bryce, you've got to come up here!"

Yeah, I could just hear it: "Bryce and Juli sitting in a tree . . ." Was I ever going to leave the second grade behind?

24 One morning I was specifically *not* looking up when out of nowhere she swings down from a branch and practically knocks me over. Heart a-ttack! I dropped my backpack and wrenched my neck, and that did it. I refused to wait under that tree with that maniac monkey on the loose anymore. I started leaving the house at the very last minute. I made up my own waiting spot, and when I'd see the bus pull up, I'd truck up the hill and get on board.

No Juli, no problem.

And that, my friend, took care of the rest of seventh grade and almost all of eighth, too, until one day a few months ago. That's when I heard a commotion up the hill and could see some big trucks parked up on Collier Street where the bus pulls in. There were some men shouting stuff up at Juli, who was, of course, five stories up in the tree.

All the other kids started to gather under the tree,

too, and I could hear them telling her she had to come down. She was fine—that was obvious to anyone with a pair of ears—but I couldn't figure out what they were all arguing about.

I trucked up the hill, and as I got closer and saw what the men were holding, I figured out in a hurry what was making Juli refuse to come out of the tree.

Chain saws.

Don't get me wrong here, okay? The tree was an ugly mutant tangle of gnarly branches. The girl arguing with those men was Juli—the world's peskiest, bossiest, most know-it-all female. But all of a sudden my stomach completely bailed on me. Juli loved that tree. Stupid as it was, she loved that tree, and cutting it down would be like cutting out her heart.

Everyone tried to talk her down. Even me. But she said she wasn't coming down, not ever, and then she tried to talk us *up*. "Bryce, please! Come up here with me. They won't cut it down if we're all up here!"

For a second I considered it. But then the bus arrived and I talked myself out of it. It wasn't my tree, and even though she acted like it was, it wasn't Juli's, either.

We boarded the bus and left her behind, but school was pretty much a waste. I couldn't seem to stop thinking about Juli. Was she still up in the tree? Were they going to arrest her?

When the bus dropped us off that afternoon, Juli was gone and so was half the tree. The top branches, the place my kite had been stuck, her favorite perch—they were all gone.

25

We watched them work for a little while, the chain saws gunning at full throttle, smoking as they chewed through wood. The tree looked lopsided and naked, and after a few minutes I had to get out of there. It was like watching someone dismember a body, and for the first time in ages, I felt like crying. *Crying.* Over a stupid tree that I hated.

I went home and tried to shake it off, but I kept wondering, Should I have gone up the tree with her? Would it have done any good?

I thought about calling Juli to tell her I was sorry they'd cut it down, but I didn't. It would've been too, I don't know, weird.

26

She didn't show at the bus stop the next morning and didn't ride the bus home that afternoon, either.

Then that night, right before dinner, my grandfather summoned me into the front room. He didn't call to me as I was walking by—that would have bordered on friendliness. What he did was talk to my mother, who talked to me. "I don't know what it's about, honey," she said. "Maybe he's just ready to get to know you a little better."

Great. The man's had a year and a half to get acquainted, and he chooses now to get to know me. But I couldn't exactly blow him off.

My grandfather's a big man with a meaty nose and greased-back salt-and-pepper hair. He lives in house slippers and a sports coat, and I've never seen a whisker on him. They grow, but he shaves them off like three times a day. It's a real recreational activity for him.

Besides his meaty nose, he's also got big meaty

hands. I suppose you'd notice his hands regardless, but what makes you realize just how beefy they are is his wedding ring. That thing's never going to come off, and even though my mother says that's how it should be, I think he ought to get it cut off. Another few pounds and that ring's going to amputate his finger.

When I went in to see him, those big hands of his were woven together, resting on the newspaper in his lap. I said, "Granddad? You wanted to see me?"

"Have a seat, son."

Son? Half the time he didn't seem to know who I was, and now suddenly I was "son"? I sat in the chair opposite him and waited.

"Tell me about your friend Juli Baker."

"*Juli?* She's not exactly my friend...!"

"Why *is* that?" he asked. Calmly. Like he had prior knowledge.

I started to justify it, then stopped myself and asked, "Why do you want to know?"

He opened the paper and pressed down the crease, and that's when I realized that Juli Baker had made the front page of the *Mayfield Times*. There was a huge picture of her in the tree, surrounded by a fire brigade and policemen, and then some smaller photos I couldn't make out very well. "Can I see that?"

He folded it up but didn't hand it over. "Why isn't she your friend, Bryce?"

"Because she's..." I shook my head and said, "You'd have to know Juli."

"I'd like to."

"What? Why?"

"Because the girl's got an iron backbone. Why don't you invite her over sometime?"

"An iron backbone? Granddad, you don't understand! That girl is a royal *pain*. She's a show-off, she's a know-it-all, and she is pushy beyond belief!"

"Is that so."

"Yes! That's absolutely so! And she's been stalking me since the second grade!"

He frowned, then looked out the window and asked, "They've lived there that long?"

"I think they were all born there!"

He frowned some more before he looked back at me and said, "A girl like that doesn't live next door to everyone, you know."

"Lucky them!"

He studied me, long and hard. I said, "What?" but he didn't flinch. He just kept staring at me, and I couldn't take it—I had to look away.

Keep in mind that this was the first real conversation I'd had with my grandfather. This was the first time he'd made the effort to talk to me about something besides passing the salt. And does he want to get to know me? No! He wants to know about Juli!

I couldn't just stand up and leave, even though that's what I felt like doing. Somehow I knew if I left like that, he'd quit talking to me at all. Even about salt. So I sat there feeling sort of tortured. Was he mad at me? How could he be mad at me? I hadn't done anything wrong!

When I looked up, he was sitting there holding out the newspaper to me. "Read this," he said. "Without prejudice."

I took it, and when he went back to looking out the window, I knew—I'd been dismissed.

By the time I got down to my room, I was mad. I slammed my bedroom door and flopped down on the bed, and after fuming about my sorry excuse for a grandfather for a while, I shoved the newspaper in the bottom drawer of my desk. Like I needed to know any more about Juli Baker.

At dinner my mother asked me why I was so sulky, and she kept looking from me to my grandfather. Granddad didn't seem to need any salt, which was a good thing because I might have thrown the shaker at him.

My sister and dad were all business as usual, though. Lynetta ate about two raisins out of her carrot salad, then peeled the skin and meat off her chicken wing and nibbled gristle off the bone, while my father filled up airspace talking about office politics and the need for a shakedown in upper management.

No one was listening to him—no one ever does when he gets on one of his if-I-ran-the-circus jags—but for once Mom wasn't even pretending. And for once she wasn't trying to convince Lynetta that dinner was delicious either. She just kept eyeing me and Granddad, trying to pick up on why we were miffed at each other.

Not that he had anything to be miffed at *me* about. What had I done to him, anyway? Nothing. Nada. But he was, I could tell. And I completely avoided looking at him until about halfway through dinner, when I sneaked a peek.

He was studying me, all right. And even though it

wasn't a mean stare, or a hard stare, it was, you know, firm. Steady. And it weirded me out. What was his deal?

I didn't look at him again. Or at my mother. I just went back to eating and pretended to listen to my dad. And the first chance I got, I excused myself and holed up in my room.

I was planning to call my friend Garrett like I usually do when I'm bent about something. I even punched in his number, but I don't know. I just hung up.

And later when my mom came in, I faked like I was sleeping. I haven't done that in years. The whole night was weird like that. I just wanted to be left alone.

Juli wasn't at the bus stop the next morning. Or Friday morning. She was at school, but you'd never know it if you didn't actually look. She didn't whip her hand through the air trying to get the teacher to call on her or charge through the halls getting to class. She didn't make unsolicited comments for the teacher's edification or challenge the kids who took cuts in the milk line. She just sat. Quiet.

I told myself I should be glad about it—it was like she wasn't even there, and isn't that what I'd always wanted? But still, I felt bad. About her tree, about how she hurried off to eat by herself in the library at lunch, about how her eyes were red around the edges. I wanted to tell her, Man, I'm sorry about your sycamore tree, but the words never seemed to come out.

By the middle of the next week, they'd finished taking down the tree. They cleared the lot and even tried to pull up the stump, but that sucker would not budge, so they wound up grinding it down into the dirt.

Juli still didn't show at the bus stop, and by the end of the week I learned from Garrett that she was riding a bike. He said he'd seen her on the side of the road twice that week, putting the chain back on the derailleur of a rusty old ten-speed.

I figured she'd be back. It was a long ride out to Mayfield Junior High, and once she got over the tree, she'd start riding the bus again. I even caught myself looking for her. Not on the lookout, just looking.

Then one day it rained and I thought for sure she'd be up at the bus stop, but no. Garrett said he saw her trucking along on her bike in a bright yellow poncho, and in math I noticed that her pants were still soaked from the knees down.

When math let out, I started to chase after her to tell her that she ought to try riding the bus again, but I stopped myself in the nick of time. What was I thinking? That Juli wouldn't take a little friendly concern and completely misinterpret it? Whoa now, buddy, beware! Better to just leave well enough alone.

After all, the last thing I needed was for Juli Baker to think I missed her.

31

The Sycamore Tree

I love to watch my father paint. Or really, I love to hear him talk while he paints. The words always come out soft and somehow heavy when he's brushing on the layers of a landscape. Not sad. Weary, maybe, but peaceful.

My father doesn't have a studio or anything, and since the garage is stuffed with things that everyone thinks they need but no one ever uses, he paints outside.

Outside *is* where the best landscapes are, only they're nowhere near our house. So what he does is keep a camera in his truck. His job as a mason takes him to lots of different locations, and he's always on the lookout for a great sunrise or sunset, or even just a nice field with sheep or cows. Then he picks out one of the snapshots, clips it to his easel, and paints.

The paintings come out fine, but I've always felt a little sorry for him, having to paint beautiful scenes in our backyard, which is not exactly picturesque. It never was much of a yard, but after I started raising chickens, things didn't exactly improve.

Dad doesn't seem to see the backyard or the chickens when he's painting, though. It's not just the snapshot or the canvas he sees either. It's something much bigger. He gets this look in his eye like he's transcended the yard, the neighborhood, the world. And as his big, callused hands sweep a tiny brush against the canvas, it's almost like his body has been possessed by some graceful spiritual being.

When I was little, my dad would let me sit beside him on the porch while he painted, as long as I'd be quiet. I don't do quiet easily, but I discovered that after five or ten minutes without a peep, *he'd* start talking.

I've learned a lot about my dad that way. He told me all sorts of stories about what he'd done when he was my age, and other things, too—like how he got his first job delivering hay, and how he wished he'd finished college.

When I got a little older, he still talked about himself and his childhood, but he also started asking questions about me. What were we learning at school? What book was I currently reading? What did I think about this or that.

Then one time he surprised me and asked me about Bryce. Why was I so crazy about Bryce?

I told him about his eyes and his hair and the way his cheeks blush, but I don't think I explained it very well because when I was done Dad shook his head and told me in soft, heavy words that I needed to start looking at the whole landscape.

I didn't really know what he meant by that, but it made me want to argue with him. How could he possibly understand about Bryce? He didn't know him!

But this was not an arguing spot. Those were scattered throughout the house, but not out here.

We were both quiet for a record-breaking amount of time

33

before he kissed me on the forehead and said, "Proper lighting is everything, Julianna."

Proper lighting? What was that supposed to mean? I sat there wondering, but I was afraid that by asking I'd be admitting that I wasn't mature enough to understand, and for some reason it felt obvious. Like I should understand.

After that he didn't talk so much about events as he did about ideas. And the older I got, the more philosophical he seemed to get. I don't know if he really *got* more philosophical or if he just thought I could handle it now that I was in the double digits.

Mostly the things he talked about floated around me, but once in a while something would happen and I would understand exactly what he had meant. "A painting is more than the sum of its parts," he would tell me, and then go on to explain how the cow by itself is just a cow, and the meadow by itself is just grass and flowers, and the sun peeking through the trees is just a beam of light, but put them all together and you've got magic.

I understood what he was saying, but I never *felt* what he was saying until one day when I was up in the sycamore tree.

The sycamore tree had been at the top of the hill forever. It was on a big vacant lot, giving shade in the summer and a place for birds to nest in the spring. It had a built-in slide for us, too. Its trunk bent up and around in almost a complete spiral, and it was so much fun to ride down. My mom told me she thought the tree must have been damaged as a sapling but survived, and now, maybe a hundred years later, it was still there, the biggest tree she'd ever seen. "A testimony to endurance" is what she called it.

34

I had always played in the tree, but I didn't become a serious climber until the fifth grade, when I went up to rescue a
kite that was stuck in its branches. I'd first spotted the kite
floating free through the air and then saw it dive-bomb somewhere up the hill by the sycamore tree.

I've flown kites before and I know—sometimes they're
gone forever, and sometimes they're just waiting in the middle
of the road for you to rescue them. Kites can be lucky or they
can be ornery. I've had both kinds, and a lucky kite is definitely worth chasing after.

This kite looked lucky to me. It wasn't anything fancy, just
an old-fashioned diamond with blue and yellow stripes. But it
stuttered along in a friendly way, and when it dive-bombed, it
seemed to do so from exhaustion as opposed to spite. Ornery
kites dive-bomb out of spite. They never get exhausted because
they won't stay up long enough to poop out. Thirty feet up
they just sort of smirk at you and crash for the fun of it.

So Champ and I ran up to Collier Street, and after scout-
ing out the road, Champ started barking at the sycamore tree.
I looked up and spotted it, too, flashing blue and yellow
through the branches.

It was a long ways up, but I thought I'd give it a shot. I
shinnied up the trunk, took a shortcut across the slide, and
started climbing. Champ kept a good eye on me, barking me
along, and soon I was higher than I'd ever been. But still the
kite seemed forever away.

Then below me I noticed Bryce coming around the corner
and through the vacant lot. And I could tell from the way he
was looking up that this was *his* kite.

What a lucky, *lucky* kite this was turning out to be!

JULIANNA

35

"Can you climb that high?" he called up to me.

"Sure!" I called back. And up, up, up I went!

The branches were strong, with just the right amount of intersections to make climbing easy. And the higher I got, the more amazed I was by the view. I'd never seen a view like that! It was like being in an airplane above all the rooftops, above the other trees. Above the world!

Then I looked down. Down at Bryce. And suddenly I got dizzy and weak in the knees. I was miles off the ground! Bryce shouted, "Can you reach it?"

I caught my breath and managed to call down, "No problem!" then forced myself to concentrate on those blue and yellow stripes, to focus on them and only them as I shinnied up, up, up. Finally I touched it; I grasped it; I had the kite in my hand!

36

But the string was tangled in the branches above and I couldn't seem to pull it free. Bryce called, "Break the string!" and somehow I managed to do just that.

When I had the kite free, I needed a minute to rest. To recover before starting down. So instead of looking at the ground below me, I held on tight and looked out. Out across the rooftops.

That's when the fear of being up so high began to lift, and in its place came the most amazing feeling that I was flying. Just soaring above the earth, sailing among the clouds.

Then I began to notice how wonderful the breeze smelled. It smelled like...sunshine. Like sunshine and wild grass and pomegranates and rain! I couldn't stop breathing it in, filling my lungs again and again with the sweetest smell I'd ever known.

J U L I A N N A

Bryce called up, "Are you stuck?" which brought me down to earth. Carefully I backed up, prized stripes in hand, and as I worked my way down, I could see Bryce circling the tree, watching me to make sure I was okay.

By the time I hit the slide, the heady feeling I'd had in the tree was changing into the heady realization that Bryce and I were alone.

Alone!

My heart was positively racing as I held the kite out to him. But before he could take it, Champ nudged me from behind and I could feel his cold, wet nose against my skin.

Against my skin?!

I grabbed my jeans in back, and that's when I realized the seat of my pants was ripped wide open.

Bryce laughed a little nervous laugh, so I could tell he knew, and for once mine were the cheeks that were beet red. He took his kite and ran off, leaving me to inspect the damage.

I did eventually get over the embarrassment of my jeans, but I never got over the view. I kept thinking of what it felt like to be up so high in that tree. I wanted to see it, to feel it, again. And again.

It wasn't long before I wasn't afraid of being up so high and found the spot that became *my* spot. I could sit there for hours, just looking out at the world. Sunsets were amazing. Some days they'd be purple and pink, some days they'd be a blazing orange, setting fire to clouds across the horizon.

It was on a day like that when my father's notion of the whole being greater than the sum of its parts moved from my head to my heart. The view from my sycamore was more than rooftops and clouds and wind and colors combined.

JULIANNA

It was magic.

And I started marveling at how I was feeling both humble and majestic. How was that possible? How could I be so full of peace and full of wonder? How could this simple tree make me feel so complex? So *alive*.

I went up the tree every chance I got. And in junior high that became almost every day because the bus to our school picks up on Collier Street, right in front of the sycamore tree.

At first I just wanted to see how high I could get before the bus pulled up, but before long I was leaving the house early so I could get clear up to my spot to see the sun rise, or the birds flutter about, or just the other kids converge on the curb.

I tried to convince the kids at the bus stop to climb up with me, even a little ways, but all of them said they didn't want to get dirty. Turn down a chance to feel magic for fear of a little dirt? I couldn't believe it.

I'd never told my mother about climbing the tree. Being the truly sensible adult that she is, she would have told me it was too dangerous. My brothers, being brothers, wouldn't have cared.

That left my father. The one person I knew would understand. Still, I was afraid to tell him. He'd tell my mother and pretty soon they'd insist that I stop. So I kept quiet, kept climbing, and felt a somewhat lonely joy as I looked out over the world.

Then a few months ago I found myself talking to the tree. An entire conversation, just me and a tree. And on the climb down I felt like crying. Why didn't I have someone real to talk to? Why didn't I have a best friend like everyone else seemed to? Sure, there were kids I knew at school, but none of them

38

were close friends. They'd have no interest in climbing the tree. In smelling the sunshine.

That night after dinner my father went outside to paint. In the cold of the night, under the glare of the porch light, he went out to put the finishing touches on a sunrise he'd been working on.

I got my jacket and went out to sit beside him, quiet as a mouse.

After a few minutes he said, "What's on your mind, sweetheart?"

In all the times I'd sat out there with him, he'd never asked me that. I looked at him but couldn't seem to speak.

He mixed two hues of orange together, and very softly he said, "Talk to me."

I sighed so heavily it surprised even me. "I understand why you come out here, Dad."

He tried kidding me. "Would you mind explaining it to your mother?"

"Really, Dad. I understand now about the whole being greater than the sum of the parts."

He stopped mixing. "You do? What happened? Tell me about it!"

So I told him about the sycamore tree. About the view and the sounds and the colors and the wind, and how being up so high felt like flying. Felt like magic.

He didn't interrupt me once, and when my confession was through, I looked at him and whispered, "Would you climb up there with me?"

He thought about this a long time, then smiled and said, "I'm not much of a climber anymore, Julianna, but I'll give it

39

JULIANNA

a shot, sure. How about this weekend, when we've got lots of daylight to work with?"

"Great!"

I went to bed so excited that I don't think I slept more than five minutes the whole night. Saturday was right around the corner. I couldn't wait!

The next morning I raced to the bus stop extra early and climbed the tree. I caught the sun rising through the clouds, sending streaks of fire from one end of the world to the other. And I was in the middle of making a mental list of all the things I was going to show my father when I heard a noise below.

I looked down, and parked right beneath me were two trucks. Big trucks. One of them was towing a long, empty trailer, and the other had a cherry picker on it—the kind they use to work on overhead power lines and telephone poles.

There were four men standing around talking, drinking from thermoses, and I almost called down to them, "I'm sorry, but you can't park there....That's a bus stop!" But before I could, one of the men reached into the back of a truck and started unloading tools. Gloves. Ropes. A chain. Earmuffs. And then chain saws. Three chain saws.

And still I didn't get it. I kept looking around for what it was they could possibly be there to cut down. Then one of the kids who rides the bus showed up and started talking to them, and pretty soon he was pointing up at me.

One of the men called, "Hey! You better come down from there. We gotta take this thing down."

I held on to the branch tight, because suddenly it felt as though I might fall. I managed to choke out, "The *tree*?"

JULIANNA

"Yeah, now come on down."

"But who told you to cut it down?"

"The owner!" he called back.

"But *why?*"

Even from forty feet up I could see him scowl. "Because he's gonna build himself a house, and he can't very well do that with this tree in the way. Now come on, girl, we've got work to do!"

By that time most of the kids had gathered for the bus. They weren't saying anything to me, just looking up at me and turning from time to time to talk to each other. Then Bryce appeared, so I knew the bus was about to arrive. I searched across the rooftops and sure enough, there it was, less than four blocks away.

My heart was crazy with panic. I didn't know what to do! I couldn't leave and let them cut down the tree! I cried, "You can't cut it down! You just can't!"

One of the men shook his head and said, "I am this close to calling the police. You are trespassing and obstructing progress on a contracted job. Now are you going to come down or are we going to cut you down?"

The bus was three blocks away. I'd never missed school for any reason other than legitimate illness, but I knew in my heart that I was going to miss my ride. "You're going to have to cut me down!" I yelled. Then I had an idea. They'd never cut it down if all of us were in the tree. They'd have to listen! "Hey, guys!" I called to my classmates. "Get up here with me! They can't cut it down if we're all up here! Marcia! Tony! Bryce! C'mon, you guys, don't let them do this!"

They just stood there, staring up at me.

I could see the bus, one block away. "Come *on*, you guys! You don't have to come up this high. Just a little ways. Please!"

The bus blasted up and pulled to the curb in front of the trucks, and when the doors folded open, one by one my classmates climbed on board.

What happened after that is a bit of a blur. I remember the neighbors gathering, and the police with megaphones. I remember the fire brigade, and some guy saying it was his blasted tree and I'd darn well better get out of it.

Somebody tracked down my mother, who cried and pleaded and acted not at all the way a sensible mother should, but I was not coming down. I was *not* coming down.

Then my father came racing up. He jumped out of his pickup truck, and after talking with my mother for a few minutes, he got the guy in the cherry picker to give him a lift up to where I was. After that it was all over. I started crying and tried to get him to look out over the rooftops, but he wouldn't. He said that no view was worth his little girl's safety.

He got me down and he took me home, only I couldn't stay there. I couldn't stand the sound of chain saws in the distance.

So Dad took me with him to work, and while he put up a block wall, I sat in his truck and cried.

I must've cried for two weeks straight. Oh, sure, I went to school and I functioned the best I could, but I didn't go there on the bus. I started riding my bike instead, taking the long way so I wouldn't have to go up to Collier Street. Up to a pile of sawdust that used to be the earth's most magnificent sycamore tree.

Then one evening when I was locked up in my room, my

father came in with something under a towel. I could tell it was a painting because that's how he transports the important ones when he shows them in the park. He sat down, resting the painting on the floor in front of him. "I always liked that tree of yours," he said. "Even before you told me about it."

"Oh, Dad, it's okay. I'll get over it."

"No, Julianna. No, you won't."

I started crying. "It was just a tree...."

"I never want you to convince yourself of that. You and I both know it isn't true."

"But Dad..."

"Bear with me a minute, would you?" He took a deep breath. "I want the spirit of that tree to be with you always. I want you to remember how you felt when you were up there." He hesitated a moment, then handed me the painting. "So I made this for you."

I pulled off the towel, and there was my tree. My beautiful, majestic sycamore tree. Through the branches he'd painted the fire of sunrise, and it seemed to me I could feel the wind. And way up in the tree was a tiny girl looking off into the distance, her cheeks flushed with wind. With joy. With magic.

"Don't cry, Julianna. I want it to help you, not hurt you."

I wiped the tears from my cheeks and gave a mighty sniff. "Thank you, Daddy," I choked out. "Thank you."

I hung the painting across the room from my bed. It's the first thing I see every morning and the last thing I see every night. And now that I can look at it without crying, I see more than the tree and what being up in its branches meant to me.

I see the day that my view of things around me started changing.

JULIANNA

Brawk-Brawk-Brawk!

Eggs scare me. Chickens, too. And buddy, you can laugh at that all you want, but I'm being dead serious here.

It started in the sixth grade with eggs.

And a snake.

44   And the Baker brothers.

The Baker brothers' names are Matt and Mike, but even now I can't tell you which one's which. You never see one without the other. And even though they're not twins, they do look and *sound* pretty much the same, and they're both in Lynetta's class, so maybe one of them got held back.

Although I can't exactly see a teacher voluntarily having either of those maniacs two years in a row.

Regardless, Matt and Mike are the ones who taught me that snakes eat eggs. And when I say they eat eggs, I'm talking they eat them raw and shell-on whole.

I probably would've gone my entire life without this little bit of reptilian trivia if it hadn't been for Lynetta. Lynetta had this major-league thing for Skyler Brown, who lives about three blocks down, and every chance she got, she went down there to hang out while he practiced the drums. Well, boom-boom-whap, what did I care, right? But then Skyler and Juli's brothers formed a band, which they named Mystery Pisser.

When my mom heard about it, she completely wigged out. "What kind of parents would allow their children to be in a band named Mystery Pisser? It's vile. It's disgusting!"

"That's the whole point, Mom," Lynetta tried to explain. "It doesn't mean anything. It's just to get a rise out of old people."

"Are you calling me *old,* young lady? Because it's certainly getting a rise out of me!"

Lynetta just shrugged, implying that my mom could draw her own conclusion.

"Go! Go to your room," my mother snapped.

"For what?" Lynetta snapped back. "I didn't say a thing!"

"You know perfectly well what for. Now you go in there and adjust your attitude, young lady!"

So Lynetta got another one of her teenage time-outs, and after that any time Lynetta was two minutes late coming home for dinner, my mother would messenger me down to Skyler's house to drag her home. It might have been embarrassing for Lynetta, but it was worse for me. I was still in elementary school, and the Mystery Pisser guys were in high school. They were ripe and ragged, raging power chords through the neighborhood, while I looked like I'd just gotten back from Sunday school.

I'd get so nervous going down there that my voice would squeak when I'd tell Lynetta it was time for dinner. It literally squeaked. But after a while the band dropped Mystery from their name, and Pisser and its entourage got used to me showing up. And instead of glaring at me, they started saying stuff like, "Hey, baby brother, come on in!" "Hey, Brycie boy, wanna jam?"

This, then, is how I wound up in Skyler Brown's garage, surrounded by high school kids, watching a boa constrictor swallow eggs. Since I'd already seen it down a rat in the Baker brothers' bedroom, Pisser had lost at least some of the element of surprise. Plus, I picked up on the fact that they'd been saving this little show to freak me out, and I really didn't want to give them the satisfaction.

46

This wasn't easy, though, because watching a snake swallow an egg is actually much creepier than you might think. The boa opened its mouth to an enormous size, then just took the egg in and *glub*! We could see it roll down its throat.

But that wasn't all. After the snake had glubbed down three eggs, Matt-or-Mike said, "So, Brycie boy, how's he gonna digest those?"

I shrugged and tried not to squeak when I answered, "Stomach acid?"

He shook his head and pretended to confide, "He needs a tree. Or a leg." He grinned at me. "Wanna volunteer yours?"

I backed away a little. I could just see that monster try to swallow my leg whole as an after-egg chaser. "N-no!"

He laughed and pointed at the boa slithering across the room. "Aw, too bad. He's going the other way. He's gonna use the piano instead!"

The piano! What kind of snake was this? How could

my sister stand being in the same room as these dementos? I looked at her, and even though she was pretending to be cool with the snake, I know Lynetta— she was totally creeped out by it.

The snake wrapped itself around the piano leg about three times, and then Matt-or-Mike put his hands up and said, "Shhh! Shhh! Everybody quiet. Here goes!"

The snake stopped moving, then flexed. And as it flexed, we could hear the eggs crunch inside him. "Oh, gross!" the girls wailed. "Whoa, dude!" the guys all said. Mike and Matt smiled at each other real big and said, "Dinner is served!"

I tried to act cool about the snake, but the truth is I started having bad dreams about the thing swallowing eggs. And rats. And cats.

And *me*.

Then the real-life nightmare began.

One morning about two weeks after the boa show in Skyler's garage, Juli appears on our doorstep, and what's she got in her hands? A half-carton of eggs. She bounces around like it's Christmas, saying, "Hiya, Bryce! Remember Abby and Bonnie and Clyde and Dexter? Eunice and Florence?"

I just stared at her. Somehow I remembered Santa's reindeer a little different than that.

"You know . . . my chickens? The ones I hatched for the science fair last year?"

"Oh, right. How could I forget."

"They're laying eggs!" She pushed the carton into my hands. "Here, take these! They're for you and your family."

47

"Oh. Uh, thanks," I said, and closed the door.

I used to really like eggs. Especially scrambled, with bacon or sausage. But even without the little snake incident, I knew that no matter what you did to *these* eggs, they would taste nothing but foul to me. These eggs came from the chickens that had been the chicks that had hatched from the eggs that had been incubated by Juli Baker for our fifth-grade science fair.

It was classic Juli. She totally dominated the fair, and get this—her project was all about watching eggs. My friend, there is not a lot of action to report on when you're incubating eggs. You've got your light, you've got your container, you've got some shredded newspaper, and that's it. You're done.

48

Juli, though, managed to write an inch-thick report, plus she made diagrams and charts—I'm talking line charts and bar charts and pie charts—about the activity of eggs. Eggs!

She also managed to time the eggs so that they'd hatch the night of the fair. How does a person do that? Here I've got a live-action erupting volcano that I've worked pretty stinking hard on, and all anybody cares about is Juli's chicks pecking out of their shells. I even went over to take a look for myself, and—I'm being completely objective here—it was boring. They pecked for about five seconds, then just lay there for five *minutes*.

I got to hear Juli jabber away to the judges, too. She had a pointer—can you believe that? Not a pencil, an actual retractable *pointer*, so she could reach across her incubator and tap on this chart or that diagram as she explained the excitement of watching eggs grow for twenty-one days. The only thing she could've done to be more overboard was put on a chicken costume, and buddy, I'm convinced—if she'd thought of it, she would have done it.

But hey—I was over it. It was just Juli being Juli, right? But all of a sudden there I am a year later, holding a carton of home-grown eggs. And I'm having a hard time not getting annoyed all over again about her stupid blue-ribbon project when my mother leans out from the hallway and says, "Who was that, honey? What have you got there? Eggs?"

I could tell by the look on her face that she was hot to scramble. "Yeah," I said, and handed them to her. "But I'm having cereal."

She opened the carton, then closed it with a smile. "How nice!" she said. "Who brought them over?"

"Juli. She grew them."

"Grew them?"

"Well, her chickens did."

"Oh?" Her smile started falling as she opened the carton again. "Is that so. I didn't know she had . . . chickens."

"Remember? You and Dad spent an hour watching them hatch at last year's science fair?"

"Well, how do we know there're not . . . *chicks* inside these eggs?"

I shrugged. "Like I said, I'm having cereal."

We all had cereal, but what we talked about were eggs. My dad thought they'd be just fine—he'd had farm-fresh eggs when he was a kid and said they were delicious. My mother, though, couldn't get past the idea that she might be cracking open a dead chick, and pretty soon discussion turned to the role of the rooster—something me and my Cheerios could've done without.

Finally Lynetta said, "If they had a rooster, don't you think we'd know? Don't you think the whole neighborhood would know?"

Hmmm, we all said, good point. But then my mom pipes up with, "Maybe they got it de-yodeled. You know—like they de-bark dogs?"

"A de-yodeled rooster," my dad says, like it's the most ridiculous thing he's ever heard. Then he looks at my mom and realizes that he'd be way better off going along with her de-yodeled idea than making fun of her. "Hmmm," he says, "I've never heard of such a thing, but maybe so."

Lynetta shrugs and says to my mom, "So just ask them, why don't you. Call up Mrs. Baker and ask her."

"Oh," my mom says. "Well, I'd hate to call her eggs into question. It doesn't seem very polite, now, does it?"

"Just ask Matt or Mike," I say to Lynetta.

She scowls at me and hisses, "Shut up."

"What? What'd I do now?"

"Haven't you noticed I haven't been going down there, you idiot?"

"Lynetta!" my mom says. Like this is the first time she's heard my sister talk to me or something.

"Well, it's true! How can he *not* have noticed?"

"I was going to ask you about that, honey. Did something happen?"

Lynetta stands up and shoves her chair in. "Like you care," she snaps, and charges down to her room.

"Oh, boy," my dad says.

50

Mom says, "Excuse me," and follows Lynetta down the hall.

When my mother's gone, my dad says, "So, son, why don't *you* just ask Juli?"

"Dad!"

"It's just a little question, Bryce. No harm, no foul."

"But it'll get me a half-hour answer!"

He studies me for a minute, then says, "No boy should be this afraid of a girl."

"I'm not *afraid* of her...!"

"I think you are."

"Dad!"

"Seriously, son. I want you to get us an answer. Conquer your fear and get us an answer."

"To whether or not they have a rooster?"

"That's right." He gets up and clears his cereal bowl, saying, "I've got to get to work and you've got to get to school. I'll expect a report tonight."

Great. Just great. The day was doomed before it had started. But then at school when I told Garrett about what had happened, he just shrugged and said, "Well, she lives right across the street from you, right?"

"Yeah, so?"

"So just go look over the fence."

"You mean spy?"

"Sure."

"But... how can I tell if one of them's a rooster or not?"

"Roosters are...I don't know...bigger. And they have more feathers."

"Feathers? Like I've got to go and count feathers?"

"No, stupid! My mom says that the male's always

brighter." Then he laughs and says, "Although in your case I'm not so sure."

"Thanks. You are giving me big-time help here, buddy. I really appreciate it."

"Look, a rooster's going to be bigger and have brighter feathers. You know, those long ones in the back? They're redder or blacker or whatever. And don't roosters have some rubbery red stuff growing off the top of their head? And some off their neck, too? Yeah, the rooster's got all sorts of rubbery red stuff all around its face."

"So you're saying I'm supposed to look over the fence for big feathers and rubbery red stuff."

"Well, come to think of it, chickens have that rubbery red stuff, too. Just not as much of it."

I rolled my eyes at him and was about to say, Forget it, I'll just ask Juli, but then he says, "I'll come with you if you want."

"Seriously?"

"Yeah, dude. Seriously."

And that, my friend, is how I wound up spying over the Bakers' back fence with Garrett Anderson at three-thirty that afternoon. Not my choice of covert operations, but a necessary one in order to report back to my dad that night at dinner.

We got there fast, too. The bell rang and we basically charged off campus because I figured if we got to the Bakers' quick enough, we could look and leave before Juli was anywhere near her house. We didn't even drop off our backpacks. We went straight down the alley and started spying.

It's not really necessary to look *over* the Bakers'

fence. You can see almost as well looking through it. But Garrett kept sticking his head up, so I figured I should too, although in the back of my mind I was aware that Garrett didn't have to live in this neighborhood—I did.

The backyard was a mess. Big surprise. The bushes were out of control, there was some kind of hodgepodge wood-and-wire coop off to one side, and the yard wasn't grass, it was highly fertilized dirt.

Garrett was the first to notice their dog, sacked out on the patio between two sorry-looking folding chairs. He points at him and says, "You think he's going to give us trouble?"

"We're not going to be here long enough to get in trouble! Where are those stupid chickens?"

"Probably in the coop," he says, then picks up a rock and throws it at the mess of plywood and chicken wire.

At first all we hear is a bunch of feathers flapping, but then one of the birds comes fluttering out. Not very far, but enough so we can see it's got feathers and rubbery red stuff.

"So?" I ask him. "Is that a rooster?"

He shrugs. "Looks like a chicken to me."

"How can you tell?"

He shrugs again. "Just does."

We watch it scratching at the dirt for a minute, and then I ask, "What's a hen, anyway?"

"A hen?"

"Yeah. You got roosters, you got chickens, and then there's hens. What's a hen?"

"It's one of those," he says, pointing into the Bakers' backyard.

"Then what's a chicken?"

He looks at me like I'm crazy. "What are you talking about?"

"Chickens! What's a chicken?"

He takes a step back from me and says, "Brycie boy, you are losin' it. *That's* a chicken!" He stoops down to pick up another rock, and he's just about to let it fly when the sliding-glass door to the back patio opens up and Juli steps outside.

We both duck. And as we're checking her out through the fence, I say, "When did she get home?"

Garrett grumbles, "While you were losing it about chickens." Then he whispers, "But hey, this'll work great. She's got a basket, right? She's probably coming out to collect eggs."

First she had to get all mushy with that mangy mutt of hers. She got down and nuzzled and ruffled and patted and hugged, telling him what a good boy he was. And when she finally let him go back to sleep, she had to stop and coo at the bird Garrett had scared out, and then she started singing. Singing. At the top of her lungs, she goes, *"I've got sunshine on a cloudy day. When it's cold outsi-ye-yide, I've got the month of May. I guess you'd say, what can make me feel this way? My girls. Talkin' 'bout my little gir-ur-rls . . ."* She looks inside the coop and coos, "Hello, Flo! Good afternoon, Bonnie! Come on out, punkin!"

The coop wasn't big enough for her to walk in. It was more like a mini lean-to shack that even her dog would have trouble crawling in. Does that stop Juli Baker? No. She gets down on her hands and knees and dives right

54

in. Chickens come squawking and flapping out, and pretty soon the yard's full of birds, and all we can see of Juli is her poop-covered shoes.

That's not all we can hear, though. She's warbling inside that coop, going, *"I don't need money, no fortune or faaa-ya-yame. I got all the riches, baby, anyone can claim. Well, I guess you'd say, what can make me feel this way? My girls. Talkin' 'bout my little gir-ur-rls, my girls..."*

At this point I wasn't checking the chickens out for rubbery red stuff or feathers. I was looking at the bottom of Juli Baker's feet, wondering how in the world a person could be so happy tunneling through a dilapidated chicken coop with poop stuck all over her shoes.

Garrett got me back on track. "They're all chickens," he says. "Look at 'em."

I quit checking out Juli's shoes and started checking out birds. The first thing I did was count them. One-two-three-four-five-six. All accounted for. After all, how could anyone forget she'd hatched six? It was the all-time school record—everyone in the county had heard about that.

But I was not really sure how to ask Garrett about what he had said. Yeah, they were all chickens, but what did that mean? I sure didn't want him coming down on me again, but it still didn't make sense. Finally I asked him, "You mean there's no rooster?"

"Correctomundo."

"How can you tell?"

He shrugged. "Roosters strut."

"Strut."

55

"That's right. And look—none of them have long feathers. Or very much of that rubbery red stuff." He nodded. "Yeah. They're definitely all chickens."

≺ ≺ ≺ ≺ ≺

That night my father got right to the point. "So, son, mission accomplished?" he asked as he stabbed into a mountain of fettuccine and whirled his fork around.

I attacked my noodles too and gave him a smile. "Uh-huh," I said as I sat up tall to deliver the news. "They're all chickens."

The turning of his fork came to a grinding halt. "And . . . ?"

56   I could tell something was wrong, but I didn't know what. I tried to keep the smile plastered on my face as I said, "And what?"

He rested his fork and stared at me. "Is that what she said? 'They're all chickens'?"

"Uh, not exactly."

"Then exactly what did she say?"

"Uh . . . she didn't exactly say anything."

"Meaning?"

"Meaning I went over there and took a look for myself." I tried very hard to sound like this was a major accomplishment, but he wasn't buying.

"You didn't ask her?"

"I didn't have to. Garrett knows a lot about chickens, and we went over there and found out for ourselves."

Lynetta came back from rinsing the Romano sauce off her seven and a half noodles, then reached for the salt and scowled at me, saying, "You're the chicken."

"Lynetta!" my mother said. "Be nice."

Lynetta stopped shaking the salt. "Mother, he spied. You get it? He went over there and looked over the fence. Are you saying you're okay with that?"

My mom turned to me. "Bryce? Is that true?"

Everyone was staring at me now, and I felt like I had to save face. "What's the big deal? You told me to find out about her chickens, and I found out about her chickens!"

"Brawk-brawk-brawk!" my sister whispered.

My father still wasn't eating. "And what you found out," he said, like he was measuring every word, "was that they're all . . . chickens."

"Right."

He sighed, then took that bite of noodles and chewed it for the longest time.

It felt like I was sinking fast, but I couldn't figure out why. So I tried to bail out with, "And you guys can go ahead and eat those eggs, but there's no way I'm going to touch them, so don't even ask."

My mother's looking back and forth from my dad to me while she eats her salad, and I can tell she's waiting for him to address my adventure as a neighborhood operative. But since he's not saying anything, she clears her throat and says, "Why's that?"

"Because there's . . . well, there's . . . I don't know how to say this nicely."

"Just *say* it," my father snaps.

"Well, there's, you know, excrement everywhere."

"Oh, gross!" my sister says, throwing down her fork.

"You mean chicken droppings?" my mother asks.

"Yeah. There's not even a lawn. It's all dirt and, uh,

you know, chicken turds. The chickens walk in it and peck through it and..."

"Oh, gross!" Lynetta wails.

"Well, it's true!"

Lynetta stands up and says, "You expect me to eat after this?" and stalks out of the room.

"Lynetta! You have to eat something," my mother calls after her.

"No, I don't!" she shouts back; then a second later she sticks her head back into the dining room and says, "And don't expect me to eat any of those eggs either, Mother. Does the word *salmonella* mean anything to you?"

Lynetta takes off down the hall and my mother says, "Salmonella?" She turns to my father. "Do you suppose they could have salmonella?"

"I don't know, Patsy. I'm more concerned that our son is a coward."

"A coward! Rick, please. Bryce is no such thing. He's a wonderful child who's—"

"Who's afraid of a *girl*."

"Dad, I'm not afraid of her, she just bugs me!"

"Why?"

"You know why! She bugs you, too. She's over the top about everything!"

"Bryce, I asked you to conquer your fear, but all you did was give in to it. If you were in love with her, that would be one thing. Love is something to be afraid of, but this, this is embarrassing. So she talks too much, so she's too enthused about every little thing, so what? Get in, get your question answered, and get out. Stand up to her, for cryin' out loud!"

"Rick...," my mom was saying, "Rick, calm down. He did find out what you asked him to—"

"No, he didn't!"

"What do you mean?"

"He tells me they're all chickens! Of course they're all chickens! The question is how many are hens, and how many are roosters."

I could almost hear the click in my brain, and man, I felt like a complete doofus. No wonder he was disgusted with me. I was an idiot! They were all chickens... du-uh! Garrett acted like he was some expert on chickens, and he didn't know diddly-squat! Why had I listened to him?

But it was too late. My dad was convinced I was a coward, and to get me over it, he decided that what I should do was take the carton of eggs back to the Bakers and tell them we didn't eat eggs, or that we were allergic to them, or something.

Then my mom butts in with, "What are you teaching him here, Rick? None of that is true. If he returns them, shouldn't he tell them the truth?"

"What, that you're afraid of salmonella poisoning?"

"Me? Aren't you a little concerned, too?"

"Patsy, that's not the point. The point is, I will not have a coward for a son!"

"But teaching him to lie?"

"Fine. Then just throw them away. But from now on I expect you to look that little tiger square in the eye, you hear me?"

"Yes, sir."

"Okay, then."

I was off the hook for all of about eight days. Then

59

there she was again, at seven in the morning, bouncing up and down on our porch with eggs in her hands. "Hi, Bryce! Here you go."

I tried to look her square in the eye and tell her, No thanks, but she was so darned happy, and I wasn't really awake enough to tackle the tiger. She wound up pushing another carton into my hands, and I wound up ditching them in the kitchen trash before my father sat down to breakfast.

This went on for two years. Two years! And it got to a point where it was just part of my morning routine. I'd be on the lookout for Juli so I could whip the door open before she had the chance to knock or ring the bell, and then I'd bury the eggs in the trash before my dad showed up.

60

Then came the day I blew it. Juli'd actually been making herself pretty scarce because it was around the time they'd taken the sycamore tree down, but suddenly one morning she was back on our doorstep, delivering eggs. I took them, as usual, and I went to chuck them, as usual. But the kitchen trash was so full that there wasn't any room for the carton, so I put it on top, picked up the trash, and beat it out the front door to empty everything into the garbage can outside.

Well, guess who's just standing there like a statue on my porch?

The Egg Chick.

I about spilled the trash all over the porch. "What are you still doing here?" I asked her.

"I . . . I don't know. I was just . . . thinking."

"About what?" I was desperate. I needed a distraction. Some way around her with this garbage before she noticed what was sitting right there on top.

She looked away like she was embarrassed. Juli Baker embarrassed? I didn't think it was possible.

Whatever. The golden opportunity to whip a soggy magazine over the egg carton had presented itself, and buddy, I took it. Then I tried to make a fast break for the garbage can in the side yard, only she body-blocked me. Seriously. She stepped right in my way and put her arms out like she's guarding the goal.

She chased me and blocked me again. "What happened?" she wants to know. "Did they break?"

Perfect. Why hadn't I thought of that? "Yeah, Juli," I told her. "And I'm real sorry about that." But what I'm thinking is, Please, God, oh please, God, let me make it to the garbage can.

God must've been sleeping in. Juli tackled the trash and pulled out her precious little carton of eggs, and she could tell right off that they weren't broken. They weren't even cracked.

She stood frozen with the eggs in her hands while I dumped the rest of the trash. "Why did you throw them out?" she asked, but her voice didn't sound like Juli Baker's voice. It was quiet. And shaky.

So I told her we were afraid of salmonella poisoning because her yard was a mess and that we were just trying to spare her feelings. I told it to her like we were right and she was wrong, but I felt like a jerk. A complete cluck-faced jerk.

Then she tells me that a couple of neighbors have been buying eggs off her. *Buying* them. And while I'm

61

coming to grips with this incredible bit of news, she whips out her mental calculator. "Do you realize I've lost over a hundred dollars giving these eggs to you?" Then she races across the street in a flood of tears.

As much as I tried to tell myself that I hadn't asked her for the eggs—I hadn't said we wanted them or needed them or liked them—the fact was, I'd never seen Juli cry before. Not when she'd broken her arm in P.E., not when she'd been teased at school or ditched by her brothers. Not even when they'd cut down the sycamore tree. I'm pretty sure she cried then, but I didn't actually see it. To me, Juli Baker had always been too tough to cry.

I went down to my room to pack my stuff for school, feeling like the biggest jerk to ever hit the planet. I'd been sneaking around throwing out eggs for over two years, avoiding her, avoiding my father—what did that make me? Why hadn't I just stood up and said, No thanks, don't want 'em, don't need 'em, don't like 'em.... Give them to the snake, why don't you? Something!

Was I really afraid of hurting her feelings?

Or was I afraid of *her*?

The Eggs

After they cut down the sycamore tree, it seemed like everything else fell apart, too. Champ died. And then I found out about the eggs. It was Champ's time to go, and even though I still miss him, I think it's been easier for me to deal with his death than it has been for me to deal with the truth about the eggs. I still cannot believe it about the eggs.

The eggs came before the chickens in our case, but the dog came before them both. One night when I was about six years old, Dad came home from work with a full grown dog tied down in the back of his truck. Someone had hit it in the middle of an intersection, and Dad had stopped to see how badly it was hurt. Then he noticed that the poor thing was skinny as a rail and didn't have any tags. "Starving and completely disoriented," he told my mother. "Can you imagine someone abandoning their dog like that?"

The whole family had converged on the front porch, and I could hardly contain myself. A dog! A wonderful, happy, panty dog! I realize now that Champ was never much of a looker, but when you're six, any dog—no matter how mangy—is a glorious, huggable creature.

JULIANNA

He looked pretty good to my brothers, too, but from the way my mother's face was pinched, I could tell she was thinking, Abandon this dog? Oh, I can see it. I can definitely see it. What she said, though, was simply, "There is no room for that animal in this house."

"Trina," my dad said, "it's not a matter of ownership. It's a matter of compassion."

"You're not springing it on me as a . . . a pet, then?"

"That is definitely not my intention."

"Well, then what *do* you intend to do?"

"Give him a decent meal, a bath . . . then maybe we'll place an ad and find him a home."

She eyed him from across the threshold. "There'll be no 'maybe' about it."

My brothers said, "We don't get to keep him?"

"That's right."

"But Mo-om," they moaned.

"It's not open to discussion," she said. "He gets a bath, he gets a meal, he gets an ad in the paper."

My father put one arm around Matt's shoulder and the other around Mike's. "Someday, boys, we'll get a puppy."

My mother was already heading back inside, but over *her* shoulder came, "Not until you learn to keep your room neat, boys!"

By the end of the week, the dog was named Champ. By the end of the *next* week, he'd made it from the backyard into the kitchen area. And not too long after that, he was all moved in. It seemed nobody wanted a full-grown dog with a happy bark. Nobody but four-fifths of the Baker family, anyway.

JULIANNA

Then my mother started noticing an odor. A mysterious odor of indeterminate origin. We all admitted we smelled it, too, but where my mother was convinced it was Eau de Champ, we disagreed. She had us bathing him so often that it couldn't possibly be him. We each sniffed him out pretty good and he smelled perfectly rosy.

My personal suspicion was that Matt and Mike were the ones not bathing enough, but I didn't want to get close enough to sniff them. And since our camp was divided on just who the culprit or culprits were, the odor was dubbed the Mystery Smell. Whole dinnertime discussions revolved around the Mystery Smell, which my brothers found amusing and my mother did not.

Then one day my mother cracked the case. And she might have cracked Champ's skull as well if my dad hadn't come to the rescue and shooed him outside.

Mom was fuming. "I told you it was him. The Mystery Smell comes from the Mystery *Pisser*! Did you see that? Did you *see* that? He just squirted on the end table!"

My father raced with a roll of paper towels to where Champ had been, and said, "Where? Where is it?"

All of three drops were dripping down the table leg. "There," my mother said, pointing a shaky finger at the wetness. "There!"

Dad wiped it up, then checked the carpet and said, "It was barely a drop."

"Exactly!" my mother said with her hands on her hips. "Which is why I've never been able to find anything. That dog stays outside from now on. Do you hear me? He is no longer allowed in this house!"

"How about the garage?" I asked. "Can he sleep in there?"

"And have him tag everything that's out there? No!"

Mike and Matt were grinning at each other. "Mystery Pisser! That could be the name for our band!"

"Yeah! Cool!"

"Band?" my mother asked. "Wait a minute, what band?" But they were already flying down to their room, laughing about the possibilities for a logo.

My father and I spent the rest of the day sniffing out and destroying criminal evidence. My dad used a spray bottle of ammonia; I followed up with Lysol. We did try to recruit my brothers, but they wound up getting into a spray-bottle fight, which got them locked in their room, which, of course, was fine with them.

So Champ became an outside dog, and he might have been our only pet ever if it hadn't been for my fifth-grade science fair.

Everyone around me had great project ideas, but I couldn't seem to come up with one. Then our teacher, Mrs. Brubeck, took me aside and told me about a friend of hers who had chickens, and how she could get me a fertilized egg for my project.

"But I don't know anything about hatching an egg," I told her.

She smiled and put her arm around my shoulders. "You don't have to be an immediate expert at everything, Juli. The idea here is to learn something new."

"But what if it dies?"

"Then it dies. Document your work scientifically and you'll still get an A, if that's what you're worried about."

An A? Being responsible for the death of a baby chick—

that's what I was worried about. Suddenly there was real appeal in building a volcano or making my own neoprene or demonstrating the various scientific applications of gear ratios.

But the ball was in motion, and Mrs. Brubeck would have no more discussion about it. She pulled *The Beginner's Guide to Raising Chickens* from her bookshelf and said, "Read the section on artificial incubation and set yourself up tonight. I'll get you an egg tomorrow."

"But..."

"Don't worry so much, Juli," she said. "We do this every year, and it's always one of the best projects at the fair."

I said, "But...," but she was gone. Off to put an end to some other student's battle with indecision.

That night I was more worried than ever. I'd read the chapter on incubation at least four times and was still confused about where to start. I didn't happen to have an old aquarium lying around! We didn't happen to have an incubation thermometer! Would a deep-fry model work?

I was supposed to control humidity, too, or horrible things would happen to the chick. Too dry and the chick couldn't peck out; too wet and it would die of mushy chick disease. Mushy chick disease?!

My mother, being the sensible person that she is, told me to tell Mrs. Brubeck that I simply wouldn't be hatching a chick. "Have you considered growing beans?" she asked me.

My father, however, understood that you can't refuse to do your teacher's assignment, and he promised to help. "An incubator's not difficult to build. We'll make one after dinner."

How my father knows exactly where things are in our garage is one of the wonders of the universe. How he knew

67

about incubators, however, was revealed to me while he was drilling a one-inch hole in an old scrap of Plexiglas. "I raised a duck from an egg when I was in high school." He grinned at me. "Science fair project."

"A duck?"

"Yes, but the principle is the same for all poultry. Keep the temperature constant and the humidity right, turn the egg several times a day, and in a few weeks you'll have yourself a little peeper."

He handed me a lightbulb and an extension cord with a socket attached. "Fasten this through the hole in the Plexiglas. I'll find some thermometers."

"Some? We need more than one?"

"We have to make you a hygrometer."

"A hygrometer?"

"To check the humidity inside the incubator. It's just a thermometer with wet gauze around the bulb."

I smiled. "No mushy chick disease?"

He smiled back. "Precisely."

By the next afternoon I had not one, but *six* chicken eggs incubating at a cozy 102 degrees Fahrenheit. "They don't all make it, Juli," Mrs. Brubeck told me. "Hope for one. The record's three. The grade's in the documentation. Be a scientist. Good luck." And with that, she was off.

Documentation? Of what? I had to turn the eggs three times a day and regulate the temperature and humidity, but aside from that what was there to do?

That night my father came out to the garage with a cardboard tube and a flashlight. He taped the two together so that the light beam was forced straight out the tube. "Let me show

68

you how to candle an egg," he said, then switched off the garage light.

I'd seen a section on candling eggs in Mrs. Brubeck's book, but I hadn't really read it yet. "Why do they call it that?" I asked him. "And why do you do it?"

"People used candles to do this before they had incandescent lighting." He held an egg up to the cardboard tube. "The light lets you see through the shell so you can watch the embryo develop. Then you can cull the weak ones, if necessary."

"*Kill* them?"

"Cull them. Remove the ones that don't develop properly."

"But . . . wouldn't that also kill them?"

He looked at me. "Leaving an egg you should cull might have disastrous results on the healthy ones."

"Why? Wouldn't it just not hatch?"

He went back to lighting up the egg. "It might explode and contaminate the other eggs with bacteria."

Explode! Between mushy chick disease, exploding eggs, and culling, this project was turning out to be the worst! Then my father said, "Look here, Julianna. You can see the embryo." He held the flashlight and egg out so I could see.

I looked inside and he said, "See the dark spot there? In the middle? With all the veins leading to it?"

"The thing that looks like a bean?"

"That's it!"

Suddenly it felt real. This egg was *alive*. I quickly checked the rest of the group. There were little bean babies in all of them! Surely they had to live. Surely they would all make it!

"Dad? Can I take the incubator inside? It might get too cold out here at night, don't you think?"

"I was going to suggest the same thing. Why don't you prop open the door? I'll carry it for you."

For the next two weeks I was completely consumed with the growing of chicks. I labeled the eggs A, B, C, D, E, and F, but before long they had names, too: Abby, Bonnie, Clyde, Dexter, Eunice, and Florence. Every day I weighed them, candled them, and turned them. I even thought it might be good for them to hear some clucking, so for a while I did that, too, but clucking is tiring! It was much easier to hum around my quiet little flock, so I did that, instead. Soon I was humming without even thinking about it, because when I was around my eggs, I was happy.

I read *The Beginner's Guide to Raising Chickens* cover to cover twice. For my project I drew diagrams of the various stages of an embryo's development, I made a giant chicken poster, I graphed the daily fluctuations in temperature and humidity, and I made a line chart documenting the weight loss of each egg. On the outside eggs were boring, but I knew what was happening on the inside!

Then two days before the science fair I was candling Bonnie when I noticed something. I called my dad into my room and said, "Look, Dad! Look at this! Is that the heart beating?"

He studied it for a moment, then smiled and said, "Let me get your mother."

So the three of us crowded around and watched Bonnie's heart beat, and even my mother had to admit that it was absolutely amazing.

Clyde was the first to pip. And of course he did it right before I had to leave for school. His little beak cracked through, and while I held my breath and waited, he rested. And rested. Finally his beak poked through again, but almost right away, he rested again. How could I go to school and just leave him this way? What if he needed my help? Surely this was a valid reason to stay home, at least for a little while!

My father tried to assure me that hatching out could take all day and that there'd be plenty of action left after school, but I'd have none of that. Oh, no-no-no! I wanted to see Abby and Bonnie and Clyde and Dexter and Eunice and Florence come into the world. Every single one of them. "I can't miss the hatch!" I told him. "Not even a second of it!"

"So take it to school with you," my mother said. "Mrs. Brubeck shouldn't mind. After all, this was *her* idea."

Sometimes it pays to have a sensible mother. I'd just set up for the science fair early, that's what I'd do! I packed up my entire operation, posters, charts, and all, and got a ride to school from my mom.

Mrs. Brubeck didn't mind a bit. She was so busy helping kids with their projects that I got to spend nearly the entire day watching the hatch.

Clyde and Bonnie were the first ones out. It was disappointing at first because they just lay there all wet and matted, looking exhausted and ugly. But by the time Abby and Dexter broke out, Bonnie and Clyde were fluffing up, looking for action.

The last two took forever, but Mrs. Brubeck insisted that I leave them alone, and that worked out pretty great because they hatched out during the fair that night. My whole family came, and even though Matt and Mike only watched for about two minutes before they took off to look at some other demonstration, my mom and dad stuck around for the whole thing. Mom even picked Bonnie up and nuzzled her.

That night after it was all over and I was packing up to go home, Mom asked, "So do these go back to Mrs. Brubeck now?"

"Do what go back to Mrs. Brubeck?" I asked her.

"The chicks, Juli. You're not planning to raise chickens, are you?"

To be honest, I hadn't thought beyond the hatch. My focus had been strictly on bringing them into the world. But she was right—here they were. Six fluffy little adorable chicks, each of which had a name and, I could already tell, its own unique personality.

"I . . . I don't know," I stammered. "I'll ask Mrs. Brubeck."

I tracked down Mrs. Brubeck, but I was praying that she didn't want me to give them back to her friend. After all, I'd hatched them. I'd named them. I'd saved them from mushy chick disease! These little peepers were mine!

To my relief and my mother's horror, Mrs. Brubeck said they were indeed mine. All mine. "Have fun," she said, then zipped off to help Heidi dismantle her exhibit on Bernoulli's law.

Mom was quiet the whole way home, and I could tell—she wanted chickens like she wanted a tractor and a goat. "Please, Mom?" I whispered as we parked at the curb. *"Please?"*

She covered her face. "Where are we going to raise chickens, Juli? Where?"

"In the backyard?" I didn't know what else to suggest.

"What about Champ?"

"They'll get along, Mom. I'll teach him. I promise."

My dad said softly, "They're pretty self-sufficient, Trina."

But then the boys piped up with, "Champ'll piss 'em to death, Mom," and suddenly they were on a roll. "Yeah! But you won't even notice 'cause they're yellow already!" "Whoa! Yellow Already—cool name." "That could work! But wait—people might think we mean our bellies!" "Oh, yeah—forget that!" "Yeah, just let him kill the chicks."

My brothers looked at each other with enormous eyes and started up all over again. "Kill the Chicks! That's it! Get it?" "You mean like we're chick killers? Or like we *kill* the *chicks*?"

Dad turned around and said, "Out. Both of you, get out. Go find a name elsewhere."

So they scrambled out, and the three of us sat in the car with only the gentle *peep-peep-peep* from my little flock breaking the silence. Finally my mother heaved a heavy sigh and said, "They don't cost much to keep, do they?"

My dad shook his head. "They eat bugs, Trina. And a little feed. They're very low-maintenance."

"Bugs? Really? What sort of bugs?"

"Earwigs, worms, roly-polys...probably spiders, if they can catch them. I think they eat snails, too."

"Seriously?" My mother smiled. "Well, in *that* case..."

"Oh, thank you, Mom. Thank you!"

And that's how we wound up with chickens. What none of us thought of was that six chickens scratching for bugs not only gets rid of bugs, it also tears up grass. Within six months there was nothing whatsoever left of our yard.

What we also didn't think of was that chicken feed attracts mice, and mice attract cats. Feral cats. Champ was pretty good at keeping the cats out of the yard, but they'd hang around the front yard or the side yard, just waiting for him to snooze so

73

JULIANNA

they could sneak in and pounce on some tender little mousy vittles.

Then my brothers started trapping the mice, which I thought was just to help out. I didn't suspect a thing until the day I heard my mother screaming from the depths of their room. They were, it turns out, raising a boa constrictor.

Mom's foot came down in a big way, and I thought she was going to throw us out, lock, stock, and boa, but then I made the most amazing discovery—chickens lay eggs! Beautiful, shiny, creamy white eggs! I first found one under Bonnie, then Clyde—whom I immediately renamed Clydette—and one more in Florence's bed. Eggs!

I raced inside to show my mom, and after a brief moment of blinking at them, she withered into a chair. "No," she whimpered. "No more chicks!"

"They're not chicks, Mom...they're eggs!"

She was still looking quite pale, so I sat in the chair next to her and said, "We don't have a rooster...?"

"Oh." The color was coming back to her cheeks. "Is that so?"

"I've never heard a *cock-a-doodle-do*, have you?"

She laughed. "A blessing I guess I've forgotten to count." She sat up a little and took an egg from my palm. "Eggs, huh. How many do you suppose they'll lay?"

"I have no idea."

As it turns out, my hens laid more eggs than we could eat. At first we tried to keep up, but soon we were tired of boiling and pickling and deviling, and my mother started complaining that all these free eggs were costing her way too much.

Then one afternoon as I was collecting eggs, our neighbor

74

JULIANNA

Mrs. Stueby leaned over the side fence and said, "If you ever have any extra, I'd be happy to buy them from you."

"Really?" I asked.

"Most certainly. Nothing quite like free-range eggs. Two dollars a dozen sound fair to you?"

Two dollars a dozen! I laughed and said, "Sure!"

"Okay, then. Whenever you have some extras, just bring 'em over. Mrs. Helms and I got to discussing it last night on the phone, but I asked you first, so make sure you offer 'em up to me before her, okay, Juli?"

"Sure thing, Mrs. Stueby!"

Between Mrs. Stueby and Mrs. Helms three doors down, my egg overflow problem was solved. And maybe I should've turned the money over to my mother as payment for having destroyed the backyard, but one "Nonsense, Julianna. It's yours," was all it took for me to start squirreling it away.

Then one day as I was walking down to Mrs. Helms' house, Mrs. Loski drove by. She waved and smiled, and I realized with a pang of guilt that I wasn't being very neighborly about my eggs. She didn't know that Mrs. Helms and Mrs. Stueby were paying me for these eggs. She probably thought I was delivering them out of the kindness of my heart.

And maybe I should've been giving the eggs away, but I'd never had a steady income before. Allowance at our house is a hit-or-miss sort of thing. Usually a miss. And earning money from my eggs gave me this secret happy feeling, which I was reluctant to have the kindness of my heart encroach upon.

But the more I thought about it, the more I realized that Mrs. Loski deserved some free eggs. She had been a good neighbor to us, lending us supplies when we ran out unexpectedly and being late to work herself when my mother needed a ride because our car wouldn't start. A few eggs now and again … it was the least I could do.

There was also the decidedly blissful possibility of running into Bryce. And in the chilly sparkle of a new day, Bryce's eyes seemed bluer than ever. The way he looked at me — the smile, the blush — it was a Bryce I didn't get to see at school. The Bryce at school was way more protected.

By the third time I brought eggs over to the Loskis, I realized that Bryce was waiting for me. Waiting to pull the door open and say, "Thanks, Juli," and then, "See you at school."

It was worth it. Even after Mrs. Helms and Mrs. Stueby offered me more money per dozen, it was still worth it. So, through the rest of sixth grade, through all of seventh grade and most of eighth, I delivered eggs to the Loskis. The very best, shiniest eggs went straight to the Loskis, and in return I got a few moments alone with the world's most dazzling eyes.

It was a bargain.

Then they cut down the sycamore tree. And two weeks later Champ died. He'd been spending a lot of time sleeping, and even though we didn't really know how old he was, no one was really surprised when one night Dad went out to feed him and discovered he was dead. We buried him in the backyard, and my brothers put up a cross that reads:

HERE LIES THE MYSTERY PISSER
P.I.P.

I was upset and pretty dazed for a while. It was raining a lot and I was riding my bike to school to avoid having to take

76

the bus, and each day when I'd get home, I'd retreat to my room, lose myself in a novel, and simply forget about collecting eggs.

Mrs. Stueby was the one who got me back on schedule. She called to say she'd read about the tree in the paper and was sorry about everything that had happened, but it had been some time now and she missed her eggs and was worried that my hens might quit laying. "Distress can push a bird straight into a molting, and we wouldn't want that! Feathers everywhere and not an egg in sight. I'm quite allergic to the feathers myself or I'd probably have a flock of my own, but never you mind. You just bring 'em over when you're up to it. All's I wanted was to check in and let you know how sorry I was about the tree. And your dog, too. Your mother mentioned he passed away."

So I got back to work. I cleared away the eggs I'd neglected and got back into my routine of collecting and cleaning. And one morning when I had enough, I made the rounds. First Mrs. Stueby, then Mrs. Helms, and finally the Loskis. And as I stood at the Loskis' threshold, it occurred to me that I hadn't seen Bryce in the longest time. Sure, we'd both been at school, but I'd been so preoccupied with other things that I hadn't really seen him.

My heart started beating faster, and when the door whooshed open and his blue eyes looked right at me, it took everything I had just to say, "Here."

He took the half-carton and said, "You know, you don't have to give us these...."

"I know," I said, and looked down.

We stood there for a record-breaking amount of time

77

saying nothing. Finally he said, "So are you going to start riding the bus again?"

I looked up at him and shrugged. "I don't know. I haven't been up there since . . . you know."

"It doesn't look so bad anymore. It's all cleared. They'll probably start on the foundation soon."

It sounded perfectly awful to me.

"Well," he said, "I've got to get ready for school. See you there." Then he smiled and closed the door.

For some reason I just stood there. I felt odd. Out of sorts. Disconnected from everything around me. Was I ever going to go back up to Collier Street? I had to eventually, or so my mother said. Was I just making it harder?

Suddenly the door flew open and Bryce came hurrying out with an overfull kitchen trash can in his hands. "Juli!" he said. "What are you still doing here?"

He startled me, too. I didn't know what I was still doing there. And I was so flustered that I would probably just have run home if he hadn't started struggling with the trash, trying to shove the contents down.

I reached over and said, "Do you need some help?" because it looked like he was about to spill the trash. Then I saw the corner of an egg carton.

This wasn't just any egg carton either. It was my egg carton. The one I'd just brought him. And through the little blue cardboard arcs I could see eggs.

I looked from him to the eggs and said, "What happened? Did you drop them?"

"Yeah," he said quickly. "Yeah, and I'm really sorry about that."

JULIANNA

He tried to stop me, but I took the carton from the trash, saying, "All of them?" I opened the carton and gasped. Six whole, perfect eggs. "Why'd you throw them away?"

He pushed past me and went around the house to the trash bin, and I followed him, waiting for an answer.

He shook the garbage out, then turned to face me. "Does the word *salmonella* mean anything to you?"

"Salmonella? But..."

"My mom doesn't think it's worth the risk."

I followed him back to the porch. "Are you saying she won't eat them because—"

"Because she's afraid of being poisoned."

"Poisoned! Why?"

"Because your backyard is, like, covered in turds! I mean, look at your place, Juli!" He pointed at our house and said, "Just *look* at it. It's a complete dive!"

"It is not!" I cried, but the truth was sitting right across the street, impossible to deny. My throat suddenly choked closed and I found it painful to speak. "Have you...always thrown them away?"

He shrugged and looked down. "Juli, look. We didn't want to hurt your feelings."

"My feelings? Do you realize Mrs. Stueby and Mrs. Helms *pay* me for my eggs?"

"You're kidding."

"No! They pay me two dollars a dozen!"

"No way."

"It's true! All those eggs I gave to you I could've sold to Mrs. Stueby or Mrs. Helms!"

"Oh," he said, and looked away. Then he eyed me and said,

"Well, why did you just *give* them to us?"

I was fighting back tears, but it was hard. I choked out, "I was trying to be neighborly...!"

He put down the trash can, then did something that made my brain freeze. He held me by the shoulders and looked me right in the eyes. "Mrs. Stueby's your neighbor, isn't she? So's Mrs. Helms, right? Why be neighborly to us and not them?"

What was he trying to say? Was it still so obvious how I felt about him? And if he knew, how could he have been so heartless, just throwing my eggs away like that, week after week, year after year?

I couldn't find any words. None at all. I just stared at him, at the clear, brilliant blue of his eyes.

"I'm sorry, Juli," he whispered.

80

I stumbled home, embarrassed and confused, my heart completely cracked open.

Get a Grip, Man

It didn't take long for me to realize that I'd traded in my old problems with Juli Baker for a whole new set of problems with Juli Baker. I could feel her anger a mile away.

It was actually worse having her mad at me than having her harass me. Why? Because I'd screwed up, that's why. I had egg all over my face, and blaming it on her yard had done nothing to wash it off. The way she ignored me, or so obviously avoided me, was a screaming loud reminder to me that I'd been a jerk. A royal cluck-faced jerk.

Then one day I'm coming home from hanging out with Garrett after school, and there's Juli in her front yard, hacking at a shrub. She is thrashing on the thing. Branches are flying over her shoulder, and clear across the street I can hear her grunting and growling and saying stuff like, "No...you...don't! You are coming... off...whether you like it or...not!"

Did I feel good about this? No, my friend, I did not. Yeah, their yard was a mess, and it was about time someone did something about it, but c'mon—where's the dad? What about Matt and Mike? Why Juli?

Because I'd embarrassed her into it, that's why. I felt worse than ever.

So I snuck inside and tried to ignore the fact that here's my desk and here's my window, and right across the street from me is Juli, beating up a bush. Not conducive to concentration. No siree, Bob. I got all of zero homework done.

The next day at school I was trying to get up the nerve to say something to her, but I never even got the chance. She wouldn't let me get anywhere near her.

Then on the ride home I had this thought. It kind of freaked me out at first, but the more I played with it, the more I figured that, yeah, helping her with the yard would make up for my having been such a jerk. Assuming she didn't boss me too much, and assuming she didn't decide to get all gooey-eyed or something stupid like that. No, I'd go up and just tell her that I felt bad for being a jerk and I wanted to make it up to her by helping her cut back some bushes. Period. End of story. And if she still wanted to be mad at me after that, then fine. That was her problem.

My problem was, I never got the chance. I came trekking down from the bus stop to find my *grandfather* doing *my* good deed.

Now, jump back. This was not something I could immediately absorb. My grandfather did not do yard work. At least, he'd never offered to help *me* out. My grandfather lived in house slippers—where'd he get those work boots? And those jeans and that flannel shirt—what was up with those?

I crouched behind a neighbor's hedge and watched them for ten or fifteen minutes, and man, the longer I watched, the madder I got. My grandfather had already said more to her in this little slice of time than he'd said to me the whole year and a half he'd been living with us. What was his deal with Juli Baker?

I took the back way home, which involved climbing two fences and kicking off the neighbor's stupid little terrier, but it was worth it, considering I avoided the garden party across the street.

Again I got no homework done. The more I watched them, the madder I got. I was still a cluck-faced jerk, while Juli was laughing it up with my grandfather. Had I ever seen him smile? Really smile? I don't think so! But now he was knee-high in nettles, *laughing*.

At dinner that night he'd showered and changed back into his regular clothes and house slippers, but he didn't look the same. It was like someone had plugged him in and turned on the light.

83

"Good evening," he said as he sat down with the rest of us. "Oh, Patsy, that looks delicious!"

"Well, Dad," my mom said with a laugh, "your excursion across the street seems to have done you a world of good."

"Yeah," my father said. "Patsy tells me you've been over there all afternoon. If you were in the mood for home improvement projects, why didn't you just say so?"

My father was just joking around, but I don't think my grandfather took it that way. He helped himself to a cheese-stuffed potato and said, "Pass the salt, won't you, Bryce?"

So there was this definite tension between my father and my grandfather, but I think if Dad had dropped the subject right then, the vibe would've vanished.

Dad didn't drop it, though. Instead, he said, "So

why's the girl the one who's finally doing something about their place?"

My grandfather salted his potato very carefully, then looked across the table at me. Ah-oh, I thought. Ah-*oh*. In a flash I knew those stupid eggs were not behind me. Two years of sneaking them in the trash, two years of avoiding discussion of Juli and her eggs and her chickens and her early-morning visits, and for what? Granddad knew, I could see it in his eyes. In a matter of seconds he'd crack open the truth, and I'd be as good as fried.

Enter a miracle. My grandfather petrified me for a minute with his eyes but then turned to my father and said, "She wants to, is all."

A raging river of sweat ran down my temples, and as my father said, "Well, it's about time *someone* did," my grandfather looked back at me and I knew—he was not going to let me forget this. We'd just had another conversation, only this time I was definitely not dismissed.

After the dishes were cleared, I retreated to my room, but my grandfather came right in, closed the door behind him, and then sat on my bed. He did this all without making a sound. No squeaking, no clanking, no scraping, no *breathing* . . . I swear, the guy moved through my room like a ghost.

And of course I'm banging my knee and dropping my pencil and deteriorating into a pathetic pool of Jell-O. But I tried my best to sound cool as I said, "Hello, Granddad. Come to check out the digs?"

He pinched his lips together and looked at nothing but me.

84

I cracked. "Look, Granddad, I know I messed up. I should've just told her, but I couldn't. And I kept thinking they'd stop. I mean, how long can a chicken lay eggs? Those things hatched in the fifth grade! That was like, three years ago! Don't they eventually run out? And what was I supposed to do? Tell her Mom was afraid of salmonella poisoning? And Dad wanted me to tell her we were allergic—c'mon, who's going to buy that? So I just kept, you know, throwing them out. I didn't know she could've sold them. I thought they were just extras."

He was nodding, but very slowly.

I sighed and said, "Thank you for not saying anything about it at dinner. I owe you."

He pulled my curtain aside and looked across the street. "One's character is set at an early age, son. The choices you make now will affect you for the rest of your life." He was quiet for a minute, then dropped the curtain and said, "I hate to see you swim out so far you can't swim back."

85

"Yes, sir."

He frowned and said, "Don't yes-sir me, Bryce." Then he stood and added, "Just think about what I've said, and the next time you're faced with a choice, do the right thing. It hurts everyone less in the long run."

With that, *poof,* he was gone.

The next day I went to shoot some hoops at Garrett's after school, and when his mom dropped me off later that afternoon, my granddad didn't even notice. He was too busy being Joe Carpenter in Juli's front yard.

I tried to do my homework at the breakfast bar, but my mom came home from work and started being all chatty, and then Lynetta appeared and the two of them started fighting about whether Lynetta's makeup made her look like a wounded raccoon.

Lynetta. I swear she'll never learn.

I packed up my stuff and escaped to my room, which, of course, was a total waste. They've got a saw revving and wailing across the street, and in between cuts I can hear the *whack, whack, whack! whack, whack, whack!* of a hammer. I look out the window and there's Juli, spitting out nails and slamming them in place. No kidding. She's got nails lined up between her lips like steel cigarettes, and she's swinging that hammer full-arc, way above her head, driving nails into pickets like they're going into butter.

For a split second there, I saw my head as the recipient of her hammer, cracking open like Humpty Dumpty. I shuddered and dropped the curtain, ditched the homework, and headed for the TV.

They handymanned all week. And every night Granddad would come in with rosy cheeks and a huge appetite and compliment my mom on what a great cook she was. Then Saturday happened. And the last thing I wanted was to spend the day at home while my grandfather churned up dirt and helped plant Juli's yard. Mom tried to get me to do our own yard, but I would have felt ridiculous micromowing our grass with Granddad and Juli making real changes right across the street.

So I locked myself in my room and called Garrett. He wasn't home, and everybody else I called had stuff they had to do. And hitting up Mom or Dad for a ride to the

86

movies or the mall was hopeless. They'd tell me I was supposed to be doing the yard.

What I was, was stuck.

And what I wound up doing was looking out the stupid window at Juli and my grandfather. It was a totally lame thing to do, but that's what I did.

I got nailed doing it, too. By my grandfather. And he, of course, had to point me out to Juli, which made me feel *another* two inches shorter. I dropped the curtain and blasted out the back door and over the fence. I had to get out of there.

I swear I walked ten miles that day. And I don't know who I was madder at—my grandfather, Juli, or me. What was wrong with me? If I wanted to make it up to Juli, why didn't I just go over there and help? What was stopping me?

I wound up at Garrett's house, and man, I'd never been so glad to see anyone in my life. Leave it to Garrett to get your mind off anything important. That dude's the master. We went out back and shot hoops, watched the tube, and talked about hitting the water slides this summer.

And when I got home, there was Juli, sprinkling the yard.

She saw me, all right, but she didn't wave or smile or anything. She just looked away.

Normally what I'd do in that situation is maybe pretend like I hadn't seen her, or give a quick wave and charge inside. But she'd been mad at me for what seemed like ages. She hadn't said word one to me since the morning of the eggs. She'd completely dissed me in

87

math a couple days before when I'd smiled at her, trying to tell her I was sorry. She didn't smile back or nod or anything. She just turned away and never looked back.

I even waited for her outside the classroom to say something, anything, about her fixing up the yard and how bad I felt, but she ditched me out the other door, and after that anytime I got anywhere near her, she'd find some way to skate around me.

So there she was, watering the yard, making me feel like a jerk, and I'd had enough of it. I went up to her and said, "It's looking real good, Juli. Nice job."

"Thanks," she said without smiling. "Chet did most of it."

Chet? I thought. *Chet?* What was she doing, calling my grandfather by his first name? "Look, Juli," I said, trying to get on with why I was there. "I'm sorry for what I did."

She looked at me for a second, then went back to watching the water spray across the dirt. Finally she said, "I still don't get it, Bryce. Why didn't you just tell me?"

"I . . . I don't know. It was dumb. I should have. And I shouldn't have said anything about the yard, either. It was, you know, out of line."

I was already feeling better. A lot better. Then Juli says, "Well, maybe it's all for the better," and starts bouncing up and down on the balls of her feet, acting more like her old self. "Doesn't it look great? I learned so much from Chet it's amazing. You are so lucky. I don't even have grandparents anymore."

"Oh," I said, not knowing *what* to say.

"I do feel sorry for him, though. He sure misses your grandmother." Then she laughs and shakes her head, saying, "Can you believe it? He says I remind him of her."

"What?"

"Yeah," she laughs again. "That's what I said. But he meant it in a nice way."

I looked at Juli and tried to picture my grandmother as an eighth grader. It was hopeless. I mean, Juli's got long, fluffy brown hair and a nose full of freckles, where my grandmother had always been some variety of blond. And my grandmother had used powder. Puffy white powder. She'd put it on her face and in her hair, in her slippers and on her *chest*.... That woman powdered everything.

I could not see Juli coated in powder. Okay, maybe *gun*powder, but the white perfumy stuff? Forget it.

I guess I was staring, because Juli says, "Look, I didn't say it, he did. I just thought it was nice, that's all."

"Yeah, whatever. Well, good luck with the grass. I'm sure it'll come up great." Then I totally surprised myself by saying, "Knowing you, you'll get 'em *all* to hatch." I didn't say it mean or anything, I really meant it. I laughed, and then she laughed, and that's how I left her—sprinkling her soon-to-be sod, smiling.

I hadn't been in such a good mood in weeks. The eggs were finally behind me. I was absolved. Relieved. Happy.

It took me a few minutes at the dinner table to realize that I was the only one who was. Lynetta had on her usual pout, so that wasn't it. But my father's idea of saying hello was to lay into me about the lawn.

89

"No sweat," I told him. "I'll do it tomorrow."

All that got me was a scowl.

Then Mom says to my granddad, "You tired tonight, Dad?"

I hadn't even noticed him sitting there like a stone.

"Yeah," my father tosses down the table at him. "That girl working you too hard?"

My grandfather straightens his fork on his napkin and says, "'That girl' is named Juli, and no, she isn't 'working me too hard,' as you so callously put it."

"Callous? Me?" My dad laughs and says, "Developed quite a soft spot for that girl, haven't you?"

Even Lynetta let her pout go for a minute. These were fighting words and everyone knew it. Mom nudged Dad with her foot, but that only made things worse. "No, Patsy! I want to know why your father has the energy and inclination to befriend a complete stranger when he's never done so much as toss a baseball around with his own grandson!"

Well, yeah! I thought. But then I remembered—I owed my grandfather. Owed him big-time. Without thinking, I said, "Take it easy, Dad. Juli just reminds him of Grandma."

Everyone clammed up and stared at me. So I looked at my grandfather and said, "Uh... isn't that right, Granddad?"

He nodded and rearranged his fork some more.

"Of Renée?" My father looked at my mother and then at Granddad. "She can't possibly!"

My granddad closed his eyes and said, "It's her spirit that reminds me of Renée."

"Her spirit," my father says. Like he's talking to a lying kindergartner.

"Yes, her spirit." My grandfather's quiet for a minute, then asks, "Do you know why the Bakers haven't fixed up the yard until now?"

"Why? Sure. They're trash, that's why. They've got a beat-up house, two beat-up cars, and a beat-up yard."

"They are not trash, Rick. They are good, honest, hardworking people—"

"Who have absolutely no pride in how they present themselves to the rest of the world. We've lived across the street from those people for over six years, and there is no excuse for the state they're in."

"No?" My grandfather takes a deep breath and seems to weigh things in his mind for a few seconds. Then he says, "Tell me this, Rick. If you had a brother or sister or child who had a severe mental or physical handicap, what would you do?"

It was like my granddad had passed gas in church. My father's face pinched, his head shook, and finally he said, "Chet, what does that have to do with anything?"

My grandfather looks at him for a minute, then quietly says, "Juli's father has a retarded brother, and—"

My father interrupts him with a laugh. "Well, *that* explains a lot, doesn't it!"

"Explains . . . a lot?" my grandfather asks. Quietly. Calmly.

"Sure! It explains why those people are the way they are . . . !" He grins around the table at us. "Must run in the family."

Everyone looks at him. Lynetta's jaw drops, and for

91

once she's speechless. My mother says, "Rick!" but all my father can do is laugh a nervous kind of laugh and say, "It was just a joke! I mean, obviously *something's* wrong with those people. Oh, excuse me, Chet. I forgot. The girl reminds you of Renée."

"Rick!" my mother says again, only this time she's mad.

"Oh, Patsy, please. Your father's being overly dramatic, trying to make me feel bad for criticizing our neighbors because there's a retarded relative someplace. Other people have family troubles and still manage to mow their lawn. They should have a little pride in ownership, for cryin' out loud!"

My grandfather's cheeks are seriously flushed, but his voice is rock-steady as he says, "They *don't* own that house, Rick. The landlord is supposed to maintain the premises, but he doesn't. And since Juli's father is responsible for his brother, all their reserves go to his care, and obviously it doesn't come cheap."

Very quietly my mom asks, "Don't they have government facilities for that kind of thing?"

"I don't know the details, Patsy. Maybe there are no government facilities nearby. Maybe they thought a private facility was a better place for him to be."

"Still," my dad says, "there are government facilities *available,* and if they don't want to go that route, that's *their* choice. It's not our fault their family had some sort of chromosomal abnormality, and I refuse to feel guilty for wanting—"

My grandfather slams his hand on the table and half-stands as he says, "It had nothing to do with chromo-

somes, Rick! It was caused by a lack of oxygen at birth."
He brings his voice down, but it makes his words seem
even more forceful. "Juli's uncle had the umbilical cord
wrapped around his neck. Twice. One minute he was a
perfect little baby, just like your son, Bryce, and the next
he was irreversibly damaged."

My mother was suddenly hysterical. In seconds she
was bawling her eyes out, *wailing,* and my father was all
over her, trying to calm her down. It was no use. She
basically dissolved right there on the spot.

Lynetta threw her napkin down and muttered, "This
family is a joke," and took off. Then my mother bolted out
of the room, sobbing into her hands, and my father raced
after her, throwing my grandfather the wickedest look I'd
ever seen.

That left Granddad and me and a table full of cold
food. "Wow," I finally said. "I had no idea."

"You still don't," he told me.

"What do you mean?"

He sat there like granite for a minute, then leaned
across the table toward me and said, "Why do you suppose that upset your mother so much?"

"I . . . I don't know." I gave a halfhearted grin and said,
"Because she's female?"

He smiled, but just barely. "No. She's upset because
she knows that she could very well be standing in Mr.
Baker's shoes right now."

I thought about it a minute and finally asked, "Did
her brother have the cord around his neck when he was
born?"

He shook his head.

93

"Well, then..."

He leaned forward even farther and whispered, "You did."

"*I* did?"

He nodded. "Twice."

"But..."

"The doctor who delivered you was on the ball, plus apparently there was some slack in the cord, so he was able to loop it off as you came out. You didn't hang yourself coming into the world, but it could very easily have gone the other way."

If I'd been told years or even weeks ago that I'd come down the chute noosed and ready to hang, I'd have made some kind of joke about it, or more likely I'd have said, Yeah, that's nice; now can you spare me the discussion?

But after everything that had happened, I was really freaking out, and I couldn't escape the questions tidal-waving my brain. Where would I be if things had been different? What would they have done with me? From the way my dad was talking, he wouldn't have had much use for me, that's for sure. He'd have stuck me in a nuthouse somewhere, *any*where, and forgotten about me. But then I thought, No! I'm his *kid*. He wouldn't do that... would he?

I looked around at everything we had—the big house, the white carpet, the antiques and artwork and *stuff* that was everywhere. Would they have given up all the *stuff* to make my life more pleasant?

I doubted it, and man, I doubted it big-time. I'd have been an embarrassment. Something to try to forget about. How things looked had always been a biggie to my parents. Especially to my dad.

Very quietly my granddad said, "You can't dwell on what might have been, Bryce." Then, like he could read my mind, he added, "And it's not fair to condemn him for something he hasn't done."

I nodded and tried to get a grip, but I wasn't doing a very good job of it. Then he said, "By the way, I appreciated your comment before."

"What?" I asked, but my throat was feeling all pinched and swollen.

"About your grandmother. How did you know that?"

I shook my head and said, "Juli told me."

"Oh? You spoke with her, then?"

"Yeah. Actually, I apologized to her."

"Well . . . !"

"And I *was* feeling a lot better about everything, but now . . . God, I feel like such a jerk again."

"Don't. You apologized, and that's what matters." He stood up and said, "Say, I'm in the mood for a walk. Want to join me?"

Go for a walk? What I wanted to do was go to my room, lock the door, and be left alone.

"I find it really helps to clear the mind," he said, and that's when I realized that this wasn't just a walk—this was an invitation to do something together.

I stood up and said, "Yeah. Let's get out of here."

For a guy who'd only basically ever said Pass the salt to me, my granddad turned out to be a real talker. We walked our neighborhood and the next neighborhood and the *next* neighborhood, and not only did I find out that my granddad knows a lot of stuff, I found out that the guy is funny. In a subtle kind of dry way. It's the stuff he says, plus the way he says it. It's really, I don't know, cool.

As we were winding back into our own territory, we passed by the house that's going up where the sycamore tree used to be. My granddad stopped, looked up into the night, and said, "It must've been a spectacular view."

I looked up, too, and noticed for the first time that night that you could see the stars. "Did you ever see her up there?" I asked him.

"Your mother pointed her out to me one time as we drove by. It scared me to see her up so high, but after I read the article I understood why she did it." He shook his head. "The tree's gone, but she's still got the spark it gave her. Know what I mean?"

96

Luckily I didn't have to answer. He just grinned and said, "Some of us get dipped in flat, some in satin, some in gloss. . . ." He turned to me. "But every once in a while you find someone who's iridescent, and when you do, nothing will ever compare."

As we walked up to our front porch, my grandfather put his arm around my shoulder and said, "It was nice walking with you, Bryce. I enjoyed myself very much."

"Me too," I told him, and we went inside.

Right away we knew we'd stepped into a war zone. And even though no one was yelling or crying, from the look on my parents' faces I could tell there'd been a major meltdown while my granddad and I were out.

Granddad whispered to me, "I've got another fence to mend, I'm afraid," and headed into the dining room to talk to my parents.

I wanted nothing to do with that vibe. I went straight to my room, closed the door, and flopped through the darkness onto my bed.

I lay there awhile and let the dinner disaster play through my mind. And when I'd totally burned a fuse thinking about it, I sat up and looked out the window. There was a light on somewhere inside the Bakers' house and the streetlights were glowing, but the night still seemed really dense. Like it was darker than usual and, I don't know, heavy.

I leaned closer to the window and looked up into the sky, but I couldn't see the stars anymore. I wondered if Juli had ever been in the sycamore at night. Among the stars.

I shook my head. Flat, glossy, iridescent. What was up with that? Juli Baker had always seemed just plain *dusty* to me.

I snapped on my desk lamp and dug the newspaper with the article about Juli out of the drawer where I'd tossed it.

Just like I thought—they made it sound like Juli was trying to save Mount Rushmore or something. They called her a "strong voice in an urban wilderness" and "a radiant beacon, shedding light on the need to curtail continued overdevelopment of our once quaint and tranquil community."

Spare me. I mean, what's wrong with letting a guy cut down a tree on his own property so he can build a house? His lot, his tree, his decision. End of story. The piece in the paper was gag-me gush.

Except. Except for the places where they quoted

Juli. Maybe it was just in contrast to the reporter's slant or something, but Juli's parts didn't come off oh-woe-is-me like I was expecting. They were, I don't know, *deep*. Sitting in that tree was seriously philosophical to her.

And the odd thing is, it all made sense to me. She talked about what it felt like to be up in that tree, and how it, like, transcended dimensional space. "To be held above the earth and brushed by the wind," she said, "it's like your heart has been kissed by beauty." Who in junior high do you know that would put together a sentence like that? None of my friends, that's for sure.

There was other stuff, too, like how something can be so much more than the parts it took to make it, and why people need things around them that lift them above their lives and make them feel the miracle of living.

I wound up reading and re-reading her parts, wondering when in the world she started thinking like that. I mean, no kidding, Juli Baker's smart, but this was something way beyond straight A's.

A month ago if I'd read this article, I would have chucked it in the trash as complete garbage, but for some reason it made sense to me now. A lot of sense.

A month ago I also wouldn't have paid any attention to the picture of Juli, but now I found myself staring at it. Not the one of the whole scene—that was more emergency rescue equipment than Juli. The other one, on the bottom half of the page. Someone must've used a killer telephoto lens, because you can tell that she's in the tree, but it's mostly from the shoulders up. She's looking off into the distance and the wind is blowing her hair back like she's at the helm of a ship or something, sailing into the sun.

I'd spent so many years avoiding Juli Baker that I'd never really looked at her, and now all of a sudden I couldn't stop. This weird feeling started taking over the pit of my stomach, and I didn't like it. Not one bit. To tell you the truth, it scared the Sheetrock out of me.

I buried the paper under my pillow and tried to remind myself of what a pain Juli Baker was. But my mind started to wander again, and pretty soon I had that stupid paper out from under my pillow.

This was insane! What was I doing?

I made myself shut out the light and go to bed. I was slipping, man, and it was definitely time to get a grip.

99

The Yard

I'd never been embarrassed by where we lived before. I'd never looked at our house, or even our side of the street, and said, Oh! I wish we lived in the new development—those houses are so much newer, so much better! This is where I'd grown up. This was my home.

I was aware of the yard, sure. My mother had grumbled about it for years. But it was a low grumbling, not worthy of deep concern. Or so I'd supposed. But maybe I should have wondered. Why let the outside go and keep the inside so nice? It was spotless inside our house. Except for the boys' room, that is. Mom gave up on that after she discovered the snake. If they were old enough to adopt a snake, she told my brothers, they were old enough to clean their own room. Matt and Mike translated this to keep the door closed, and became quite diligent about doing just that.

Besides the yard, I also never really wondered about the money, or the apparent lack thereof. I knew we weren't rich, but I didn't feel like I was missing anything. Anything you could buy, anyway.

Matt and Mike did ask for things a lot, but even though my mother would tell them, No, boys, we just can't afford that, I took this to mean, No, boys, you don't deserve that, or, No, boys, you don't really *need* that. It wasn't until Bryce called our home a complete dive that I started really seeing things.

It wasn't just the yard. It was my dad's truck, my mother's car, the family bike that was more rust than steel, and the fact that when we did buy something new, it always seemed to come from a second-time-around store. Plus, we never went on vacation. Ever.

Why was that? My father was the hardest-working man in the world, and my mother worked for TempService doing secretarial jobs whenever she could. What was all that hard work about if this is where it got you?

Asking my parents whether we were poor seemed incredibly impolite. But as the days went by, I knew I had to ask. Just had to. Every day I'd ride home from school on our rusty bike, pull past the broken fence and patchy yard, and think, Tonight. I'll ask them tonight.

But then I wouldn't ask them. I just didn't know how.

Then one day I had an idea. A way to talk to them about it and maybe help out a little, too. And since my brothers were working at the music store that night, and nobody was saying much of anything at the table, I took a deep breath and said, "I was thinking, you know, that it wouldn't be hard to fix up the front yard if I could get some nails and a hammer and maybe some paint? And how much does grass seed cost? It can't be that much, right? I could plant a lawn, and maybe even some flowers?"

My parents stopped eating and stared at me.

"I know how to use a saw and a hammer—it could be, you know, a project."

My mother quit looking at me and stared at my father, instead.

My father sighed and said, "The yard is not our responsibility, Julianna."

"It's . . . it's not?"

He shook his head and said, "It's Mr. Finnegan's."

"Who's Mr. Finnegan?"

"The man who owns this house."

I couldn't believe my ears. "What?"

My father cleared his throat and said, "The landlord."

"You mean *we* don't own this house?"

They looked at each other, having some private wordless conversation I couldn't decipher. Finally my father said, "I didn't realize you didn't know that."

102

"But . . . but that doesn't make sense! Aren't landlords supposed to come and do things? Like fix the roof when it leaks and clear the drains when they're plugged? You always do that stuff, Dad. Why do you do it when he's supposed to?"

"Because," he sighed, "it's easier than asking him for help."

"But if—"

"And," my father interrupted me, "it keeps him from raising the rent."

"But . . ."

My mother reached over and took my hand. "Sweetheart, I'm sorry if this is a shock. I guess we always thought you knew."

"But what about the yard? Why keep up the inside but not the outside?"

My father frowned and said, "When we signed the lease, he assured us he would fix the fences, front and back, and plant sod in the front yard. Obviously that never happened." He shook his head. "It's a major undertaking, and fencing is not cheap. I can't see putting that sort of investment into a property that's not ours. Plus, it's the principle of the thing."

"But we live here," I whispered, "and it looks so bad."

My father studied me. "Julianna, what happened?"

"Nothing, Daddy," I said, but he knew I was lying.

"Sweetheart," he whispered, "tell me."

I knew what he'd say if I told him, and yet I couldn't not tell him. Not with the way he was looking at me. So I took a deep breath and said, "The Loskis have been throwing my eggs away because they were afraid they'd have salmonella because our yard is such a mess."

My father said, "Oh, that's ridiculous," but my mother gasped, "What?" Then she cried, "Did Patsy say that?"

I looked down. "No, Bryce did."

103

"But it must've been a family discussion! A boy doesn't come up with that on his own . . . !" My mother looked for all the world like a doe waiting to be shot through the heart. She covered her face with her hands and said, "I can't go on like this! Robert, things have got to change. They've just got to!"

"Trina, you know I'm doing the best I can. I'm sorry about the yard, I'm sorry about the situation. This isn't the picture I had for my life, either, but sometimes you have to sacrifice for what's right."

My mother looked up from her hands and said, "This is not right for *our* family. Your daughter is suffering because we won't fix up our own yard."

"It's not our yard."

"How can you *say* that? Robert, wake up! We have lived here for twelve years. It's not temporary anymore! If we ever

JULIANNA

want to have a decent place with our own yard, if we're going to help the kids through college or do any of the other things we've promised each other, we're going to have to move him into government care."

My father let out a deep sigh and whispered, "We've discussed this so many times, Trina. In the end you always agree that keeping him at Greenhaven is the right thing to do."

I wanted to say, Wait! What are you talking about? *Who* are you talking about? But the conversation was flying so fast and furious that I couldn't seem to break in, and it wasn't long before they were bickering so badly that it was almost like I wasn't there.

Then in the back of my mind, it clicked. Everything clicked. It was my dad's brother they were talking about. My uncle. David.

To me Uncle David was only a name. Someone my parents had explained to me, but not someone I'd ever actually met. And even though I knew my dad visited him, I never knew exactly when. He never talked about it.

Dad also thought we shouldn't talk about Uncle David to others because David was retarded. "People jump to conclusions," he'd told me. "They assume that, by association, something must also be wrong with you. Trust me, I know."

So we didn't talk about it. Not at home, not with friends. It was almost like there was no Uncle David.

Until now. Now he felt larger than life, and I could tell from their argument that he was the reason we didn't have our own house; he was the reason we didn't have nice cars or fancy things. He was the reason there always seemed to be a cloud of weariness hanging over my parents.

JULIANNA

Why did I have to bring up the yard in the first place? I'd never seen my parents fight like this. Ever. I wanted to grab them and say, Stop it! Stop it! You love each other! You do! But I just sat there with tears streaming down my face.

My mother stopped suddenly and whispered, "We should not be doing this in front of her!"

"I'm sorry, Julianna," my dad said, then reached over and held my forearm. "Don't cry. None of this is your fault. We'll work it out, I promise we will."

My mother tried to laugh through her tears, saying, "We always have, and we always will."

That night my parents came into my room and talked to me, one at a time. My father talked about his brother and how much he loved him and how he'd promised his parents he'd always take care of him. My mother talked about how much she loved my father for his strength and kind heart, about dreams and reality, and the need to count your blessings. And she made me cry all over again when she kissed me goodnight and whispered that of all her many blessings, I was her best and brightest.

I felt sorry for my father. I felt sorry for my mother. But most of all I felt lucky for me that they were mine.

And in the morning, as I rode my rusty bike out the driveway to school, I promised myself that when I got home, I'd tackle the yard. Rented or not, this was our home, and I was going to help make living here better.

As it turns out, this was easier thought than done. First it took me half an hour of rummaging through the garage to find a hammer and a box of nails, a saw, and some pruners. Then it took another half hour of standing around to figure out just

105

where to start. The actual yard was just clumps of weeds, but what about the bordering shrubs? Should I dig them up, or prune them way back? *Were* they shrubs, or just overgrown weeds? And what about the fence? Should I knock it down, or rebuild it? Maybe I should take out the front end entirely and use the wood to fix up the sides.

The longer I looked around, the more I felt like forgetting the whole thing. Why bother? It wasn't our property. Mr. Finnegan should be the one making repairs.

But then I remembered my mother's words from the night before. Surely, I thought, a few bushes and some dilapidated wood couldn't stop someone's best and brightest blessing! Surely not!

And with that, I picked up the clippers and got to work.

106   Half an hour later I was keeper of the knowledge that one bush equals many branches, and that the volume of a bush increases exponentially as it's cut and tossed into the middle of a yard. It was ridiculous! Where was I going to *put* all this stuff?

Mom came home and tried to talk me out of my mission, but I'd have none of it. Oh, no-no-no! I'd already pruned two bushes down to a respectable size, and before long she'd see — the place was going to look just dandy.

"You didn't get that stubborn streak from me," she said, but came back outside with a glass of juice and a kiss for my cheek. Good enough for me!

By the end of that first day, what I'd made was a big mess. But if chaos is a necessary step in the organization of one's universe, then I was well on my way. At least that's what I tried to tell myself when I flopped into bed that night, dead tired.

JULIANNA

And the next afternoon I was busily expanding the chaos of my little universe when I heard a deep voice say, "That's quite an undertaking, young lady."

The man standing on our sidewalk was Bryce's grandfather, I knew that much. But I'd only ever seen him outside one time. All the other times I'd seen him had been through windows— either one in their sitting room or one in their car. To me he was just a dark-haired man behind glass. Having him appear on my sidewalk was like having someone from TV step through the screen and talk to you.

"I know we've seen each other from time to time," he was saying. "I'm sorry it's taken me over a year to come introduce myself. I'm Chester Duncan, Bryce's grandfather. And you, of course, are Julianna Baker."

He stuck out his hand, so I took off my work glove and watched my hand completely disappear inside his as we shook. "Nice to meet you, Mr. Duncan," I said, thinking that this man was way bigger than he looked from the sitting-room window.

Then the strangest thing happened. He pulled his own work gloves and a pair of clippers from a back pocket and said, "Are you pruning all of these to the same height?"

"Oh," I said. "Well, yes. That is what I was thinking. Although now I don't know. Do you think it would look better to just take them out?"

He shook his head and said, "They're Australian tea shrubs. They'll prune up nicely." And with that, he put on his gloves and started clipping.

At first I didn't know what to say to this man. It was very strange to be getting his help, but from the way he was acting, it was as though I shouldn't have thought a thing of it. *Clip-*

clip-clip, he went, like this was something he really enjoyed doing.

Then I remembered what Bryce had said about our yard, and suddenly I knew why he was there.

"What's the matter?" he asked, throwing his clippings into my pile. "Did I cut it down too far?"

"N-no."

"Then why the look?" he asked. "I don't mean to make you uncomfortable. I just thought you might like a little help."

"Well, I don't. I can do this by myself."

He laughed and said, "Oh, I have no doubt about that," then got back to clipping. "You see, Julianna, I read about you in the paper, and I've lived across the street from you for over a year now. It's easy to see that you're a very competent person."

We both worked quietly for a minute, but I found myself throwing the clippings into the pile harder and harder. And before long I couldn't stand it. I just couldn't stand it! I spun on him and said, "You're here because you feel bad about the eggs, aren't you? Well, our eggs are perfectly fine! We've been eating them for nearly three years and none of us have gotten poisoned. Mrs. Stueby and Mrs. Helms seem in good health to me, too, and the fact of the matter is, if you didn't want them, you should've just told me so!"

His hands fell to his sides and he shook his head as he said, "Eggs? Poisoned? Julianna, I have no idea what you're talking about."

Inside I was so angry and hurt and embarrassed that I didn't even feel like me. "I'm talking about the eggs that I've been bringing over to your house for more than two years— eggs that my chickens laid that I could've sold! Eggs that your family has been throwing away!" I was shouting at him. Shouting at an adult, like I'd never shouted at anyone in my entire life.

His voice got very quiet. "I'm sorry. I don't know about any eggs. Who did you give them to?"

"Bryce!" My throat choked closed as I said his name again. "Bryce."

Mr. Duncan nodded slowly and said, "Well," then went back to pruning his bush. "That probably explains it."

"What do you mean?"

He sighed. "The boy still has a ways to go."

I just stared at him, not trusting myself with the words sizzling on my tongue.

"Oh, he's a very handsome boy, there's no denying that," he said with a frown. Then he snapped a branch and added, "The spitting image of his father."

I shook my head. "Why are you over here, Mr. Duncan? If you don't think I need the help and you're not feeling bad about the eggs, then why would you do this?"

"Honestly?"

I just looked at him, straight in the eye.

He nodded, then said, "Because you remind me of my wife."

"Your wife?"

"That's right." He gave me a little smile and said, "Renée would've sat up in that tree with you. She would've sat there all night."

And with those two sentences, my anger vanished. "Really?"

"Absolutely."

109

"She's . . . she died?"

He nodded. "And I miss her terribly." He tossed a branch into the heap and chuckled. "There's nothing like a head-strong woman to make you happy to be alive."

The last thing in the world I expected was to become friends with Bryce's grandfather. But by dinnertime I knew so much about him and his wife and the adventures they'd had together that it seemed like I'd known him for a very long time. Plus, all his stories made the work seem easy. When I went in for the night, the bushes were all pruned back, and except for the enormous heap in the center of the yard, things were already looking a whole lot better.

The next day he was back. And when I smiled and said, "Hi, Mr. Duncan," he smiled back and said, "Call me Chet, won't you?" He looked at the hammer in my hand and said, "I take it we're starting on the fence today?"

Chet taught me how to plumb a line for the pickets, how to hold a hammer down on the end of the handle instead of choking up on it, how to calculate an adjusted spacing for the pickets, and how to use a level to get the wood exactly verti-cal. We worked on the fence for days, and the whole time we worked we talked. It wasn't just about his wife, either. He wanted to know about the sycamore tree and seemed to under-stand exactly what I meant when I told about the whole being greater than the sum of its parts. "It's that way with people, too," he said, "only with people it's sometimes that the whole is *less* than the sum of the parts."

I thought that was pretty interesting. And the next day during school I looked around at the people I'd known since elementary school, trying to figure out if they were more or less than the sum of their parts. Chet was right. A lot of them were less.

Top of the list, of course, was Shelly Stalls. To look at her, you'd think she had everything, but there's not much solid underneath her Mount Everest hair. And even though she's like a black hole at sucking people in, it doesn't take them long to figure out that being friends with her requires fanning the flames of a wildfire ego.

But of all my classmates, the one person I couldn't seem to place was Bryce. Until recently I'd have said with absolute certainty that he was greater—far greater—than the sum of his parts. What he did to my heart was sheer, inexplicable magic.

But inexplicable was the operative word here. And as I looked across the room at him during math, I couldn't help feeling crushed all over again about how he'd thrown out my eggs. What kind of person would do that?

Then he looked my way and smiled, and my heart lurched. But I was mad at myself for it. How could I still feel this way after what he'd done?

I avoided him the rest of the day, but by the end of school there was a tornado inside me, tearing me up from one end to the other. I jumped on my bike and rode home faster than I ever had before. The right pedal clanked against the chain guard, and the whole bike rattled and squeaked, threatening to collapse into a pile of rusty parts.

The tornado, however, was still going strong when I skidded to a halt in our driveway. So I transferred pedal power into painting power. I pried open the gallon of Navajo White my dad had bought me and started slopping paint around.

JULIANNA

Chet appeared about ten minutes later. "My," he laughed, "you've got an enviable amount of energy today, don't you?"

"No," I said, brushing back some hair with the back of my hand, "I'm just mad."

He produced his own brush and an empty coffee can. "Uh-oh. Who at?"

"Myself!"

"Oh, that's a tough one. Did you do poorly on a test?"

"No! I..." I turned to him and said, "How did you fall in love with your wife?"

He poured some Navajo White into his can and smiled. "Ah," he said. "Boy problems."

"I do not have boy problems!"

He hesitated but didn't argue. Instead, he said, "I fell in love with her by mistake."

"By mistake? What do you mean?"

"I didn't intend to. At the time I was engaged to somebody else, and in no position to fall in love. Fortunately for me I saw how blind I'd been before it was too late."

"Blind?"

"Yes. My fiancée was very beautiful. She had the most magnificent brown eyes, and skin like an angel. And for a time all I could see was her beauty. But then... well, let's just say I discovered she wasn't a fraction of the person Renée was." He dipped his brush in the coffee can and stroked a picket with paint. "It's easy to look back and see it, and it's easy to give the advice, but the sad fact is, most people don't look beneath the surface until it's too late."

We were quiet a minute, but I could see Chet thinking. And from the furrow in his brow, I knew it had nothing to do with my problems. "I'm . . . I'm sorry I brought up your wife," I said.

"Oh, don't be, that's all right." He shook his head and tried on a smile. "Besides, I wasn't thinking of Renée. I was thinking of someone else. Someone who's never been able to look beneath the surface. At this point I don't suppose I even want her to."

Who was he talking about? I wanted to know! But I felt it would be crossing some line to ask, so we painted pickets in silence. At last he turned to me and said, "Get beyond his eyes and his smile and the sheen of his hair—look at what's really there."

The way he said it sent a chill through me. It was as though he knew. And suddenly I felt defensive. Was he telling me his grandson wasn't worth it?

When it was time to go in for dinner, I still didn't feel right, but at least the tornado was gone. Mom said Dad was working late, and since the boys were off with their friends, it was just the two of us. She told me that she and Dad had talked about it and that they both felt a little strange having Chet come over like he was. Maybe, she said, they should find a way to pay him for his help.

I told her I thought Chet would find that insulting, but the next day she went ahead and insulted him anyway. Chet said, "No, Mrs. Baker. It's been my pleasure to help out your daughter on this project," and wouldn't hear another word about it.

The week ended with my dad loading the back of his truck with all the clippings and scraps before he set off for work on Saturday morning. Then Chet and I spent the rest of the day hoeing up weeds and raking and readying the dirt for seeding.

It was on this last day that Chet asked, "Your family's not moving, are you?"

"Moving? Why do you say that?"

"Oh, my daughter brought up the possibility at the dinner table last night. She thought that maybe you're fixing up the house because you're getting ready to sell it."

Even though Chet and I had talked about a lot of things while we were working, I probably wouldn't have told him about Mr. Finnegan or Uncle David or why the yard was such a mess if he hadn't asked me about moving. But since he had, well, I wound up telling him everything. And it felt good to talk about it. Especially about Uncle David. It felt like blowing a dandelion into the wind and watching all the little seeds float off, up and away. I was proud of my parents, and looking around the front yard, I was proud of me, too. Just wait until I got my hands on the backyard! Then maybe I'd even paint the house. I could do it. I *could*.

Chet was pretty quiet after I told him the story, and when Mom brought us out sandwiches at lunchtime, we sat on the porch and ate without saying a word. Then he broke the silence by nodding across the street and saying, "I don't know why he doesn't just come out and say hello."

"Who?" I asked, then looked across the street to where he'd nodded. The curtain in Bryce's room moved quickly back into place, and I couldn't help asking, "Bryce?"

"That's the third time I've seen him watching."

"Really?" My heart was fluttering about like a baby bird trying to fly.

114

He frowned and said, "Let's finish up and get that seed sown, shall we? You'll want the warmth of the day to help with the germination."

I was happy to finally be planting the yard, but I couldn't help being distracted by Bryce's window. Was he watching? During the rest of the afternoon, I checked more often than I'd like to admit. And I'm afraid Chet noticed, too, because when we were all done and we'd congratulated each other on what was sure to be a fine-looking yard, he said, "He may be acting like a coward now, but I do hold out hope for the boy."

A coward? What on earth could I say to that? I just stood there with the hose in one hand and the spigot valve beneath the other.

And with that, Chet waved so long and walked across the street.

A few minutes later I saw Bryce coming down the sidewalk toward his house. I did a double take. All this time I'd thought he was inside the house watching, and he was really outside walking around? I was embarrassed all over again.

I turned my back on him and concentrated on watering the yard. What a fool I was! What a complete idiot! And I had just built up a nice head of angry steam when I heard, "It's looking good, Juli. Nice job."

It was Bryce, standing right there on our driveway. And suddenly I wasn't mad at me anymore. I was mad at him. How could he stand there like my supervisor and tell me, Nice job? He had no business saying *anything* after what he'd done.

I was about to hose him down when he said, "I'm sorry for what I did, Juli. It was, you know...wrong."

I looked at him—into those brilliant blue eyes. And I

115

tried to do what Chet had said—I tried to look past them. What was behind them? What was he thinking? Was he really sorry? Or was he just feeling bad about the things he'd said?

It was like looking into the sun, though, and I had to turn away.

I couldn't tell you what we talked about after that, except that he was nice to me and he made me laugh. And after he left, I shut off the water and went inside feeling very, very strange.

The rest of the evening I bounced back and forth between upset and uneasy. The worst part being, I couldn't really put my finger on what exactly I was upset or uneasy about. Of course it was Bryce, but why wasn't I just mad? He'd been such a...scoundrel. Or happy? Why wasn't I just happy? He'd come over to our house. He'd stood on our driveway. He'd said nice things. We'd laughed.

But I wasn't mad or happy. And as I lay in bed trying to read, I realized that upset had been overshadowed by uneasy. I felt as though someone was watching me. I got so spooked I even got up and checked out the window and in the closet and under the bed, but still the feeling didn't go away.

It took me until nearly midnight to understand what it was.

It was me. Watching me.

116

Looming Large
and Smelly

Sunday I woke up feeling like I'd been sick with the flu.
Like I'd had one of those bad, convoluted, unexplainable
fever dreams.

And what I've figured out about bad, convoluted,
unexplainable dreams of any kind is that you've just got
to shake them off. Try to forget that they ever happened.

I shook it off, all right, and got out of bed early 'cause
I had eaten almost nothing the night before and I was
starving! But as I was trucking into the kitchen, I
glanced into the family room and noticed that my dad
was sacked out on the couch.

This was not good. This was a sign of battles still in
progress, and it made me feel like an invader in my own
territory.

He rolled over and kind of groaned, then curled up
tighter under his skinny little quilt and muttered some
pretty unfriendly-sounding stuff into his pillow.

I beat it into the kitchen and poured myself a killer
bowl of corn flakes. And I was about to drown it in milk
when my mother comes waltzing in and snags it away
from me. "You are going to wait, young man," she says.
"This family is going to have Sunday breakfast together."

"But I'm starving!"

"So are the rest of us. Now go! I'm making pancakes, and you're taking a shower. Go!"

Like a shower's going to prevent imminent starvation.

But I headed down to the bathroom, and on my way I noticed that the family room was empty. The quilt was folded and back on the armrest, the pillow was gone . . . it was like I'd imagined the whole thing.

At breakfast my father didn't *look* like he'd spent the night on the couch. No bags under his eyes, no whiskers on his chin. He was decked out in tennis shorts and a lavender polo shirt, and his hair was all blown dry like it was a workday. Personally I thought the shirt looked kind of girly, but my mom said, "You look very nice this morning, Rick."

My father just eyed her suspiciously.

Then my grandfather came in, saying, "Patsy, the house smells wonderful! Good morning, Rick. Hi there, Bryce," and winked at me as he sat down and put his napkin in his lap.

"Lyn-et-ta!" my mother sang out. "Break-fast!"

My sister appeared in a triple-X miniskirt and platform shoes, with eyes that were definitely of the raccoon variety. My mother gasped, but then took a deep breath and said, "Good morning, honey. You're . . . you're . . . I thought you were going to church this morning with your friends."

"I am." Lynetta scowled and sat down.

Mom brought pancakes, fried eggs, and hash browns to the table. My father just sat there stiff as a board for a minute, but finally he shook out his napkin and tucked it into his collar.

118

"Well," my mother said as she sat down, "I have come up with a solution to our situation."

"Here it comes...," my father muttered, but my mother gave him a glare that shut him down cold.

"The solution is...," my mom said as she served herself some pancakes, "...we're going to invite the Bakers over for dinner."

My father blurts out, *"What?";* Lynetta asks, *"All* of them?"; I put in, "Are you *serious*?"; but my grandfather heaps on another fried egg and says, "That, Patsy, is a marvelous idea."

"Thanks, Dad," she says with a smile, then tells Lynetta and me, "Of course I'm serious, and yes, if Juli and the boys want to come, they'll be invited."

My sister starts cracking up. "Do you know what you're saying?"

Mom smooths the napkin into her lap. "Maybe it's about time I found out."

Lynetta turns to me and says, "She's inviting the core of Piss Poor over for dinner—oh, *this* is something I really woke up expecting!"

My father shakes his head and says, "Patsy, what purpose does this serve? So I made some stupid cracks last night. Is this the next phase in my punishment?"

"It is something we should have done years ago."

"Patsy, please. I know you feel bad about what you found out, but an awkward dinner party isn't going to change anything!"

My mother ran syrup all over her pancakes, popped the top closed, licked her finger, then locked eyes with my dad. "We are having the Bakers over for dinner."

119

And that, she didn't have to tell him, was that.

Dad took a deep breath, then sighed and said, "Whatever you want, Patsy. Just don't say I didn't warn you." He took a bite of hash browns and mumbled, "A barbecue, I suppose?"

"No, Rick. A sit-down dinner. Like we have when your clients come over."

He stopped chewing. "You're expecting them to dress up?"

Mom glared at him. "What I'm expecting is for you to behave like the gentleman I always thought you were."

Dad went back to his potatoes. Definitely safer than arguing with Mom.

Lynetta wound up eating the entire white of a fried egg and almost a whole pancake besides. Plain, of course, but from the way she was glutting and giggling as she ate, it was obvious that at least she was in a good mood.

Granddad ate plenty, even for him, but I couldn't tell what he was thinking. He was back to looking more granite than human. Me, I'd started tuning in to the fact that this dinner could be more than awkward—it could be trouble. Those rotten eggs were back from the grave, looming large and smelly right over my head.

Sure, Granddad knew, but no one else in my family did. What if it came up at dinner? I'd be dead, fried, cluck-faced meat.

Later, as I was brushing my teeth, I considered bribing Juli. Getting her on board so that nobody brought up the subject of eggs. Or maybe I could sabotage the dinner somehow. Make it not happen. Yeah, I could—I stopped myself and looked in the mirror. What kind of wimp was I, anyway? I spit and headed back to find my mom.

"What is it, honey?" she asked me as she wiped off the griddle. "You look worried."

I double-checked to make sure my dad or Lynetta wasn't lurking around somewhere, then whispered, "Will you swear to secrecy?"

She laughed. "I don't know about *that.*"

I just waited.

"What can be . . . ," she said, then looked at me and stopped cleaning. "Oh, it *is* serious. Honey, what's wrong?"

It had been ages since I'd voluntarily fessed up about something to my mom. It just didn't seem necessary anymore; I'd learned to deal with things on my own. At least, that's what I'd thought. Until now.

She touched my arm and said, "Bryce, tell me. What is it?"

I hopped up to sit on the counter, then took a deep breath and said, "It's about Juli's eggs."

"About her . . . eggs?"

"Yeah. Remember that whole chicken-hen-salmonella disaster?"

"That was quite a while ago, but sure. . . ."

"Well, what you don't know is that Juli didn't bring eggs over just that once. She's been bringing them over every week . . . or about that, anyway."

"She has? Why didn't I know about this?"

"Well, I was afraid Dad would get mad at me for not telling her we didn't want them, so I started intercepting them. I'd see her coming, get to her before she rang the bell, and then I'd toss them in the trash before anyone knew she'd been here."

"Oh, Bryce!"

"Well, I kept thinking they'd stop! How long can a stupid chicken lay eggs?"

"But I take it they have stopped?"

"Yeah. As of last week. Because Juli caught me chucking a carton in the trash outside."

"Oh, dear."

"Exactly."

"So what did you tell her?"

I looked down and mumbled, "I told her that we were afraid of salmonella poisoning because their yard was such a mess. She ran off crying, and the next thing I know, she's starting to fix up their yard."

"Oh, Bryce!"

"Exactly."

She was dead quiet for a minute; then very softly she said, "Thank you for your honesty, Bryce. It does help to explain a lot." She shook her head and said, "What that family must think of us," and got back to cleaning the griddle. "All the more reason to have them over for dinner, if you ask me."

I whispered, "You're sworn to secrecy on this whole egg thing, right? I mean, Juli told Granddad, so he knows, but I don't want this to spread to, you know, Dad."

She studied me a minute, then said, "Tell me you've learned your lesson, honey."

"I have, Mom."

"Okay, then."

I let out a big sigh of relief. "Thanks."

122

"Oh, and Bryce?"

"Yeah?"

"I'm very glad you told me about it." She kissed me on the cheek, then smiled and said, "Now, didn't I hear you promise you'd mow the lawn today?"

"Right," I said, and headed outside to trim the turf.

That evening my mother announced that the Bakers would be over Friday night at six o'clock; that the menu included poached salmon, crab risotto, and fresh steamed vegetables; and that none of us had better weasel out of being there. My dad muttered that if we were really going to do this, it would be a whole lot better to barbecue because at least that way he'd have something to do, but my mom positively smoked him with her eyes and he dropped it.

So. They were coming. And it made seeing Juli at school even more uncomfortable than usual. Not because she gushed about it or even waved and winked or something. No, she was back to avoiding me. She'd say hi if we happened to run into each other, but instead of being, like, right over my shoulder anytime I looked, she was nowhere. She must have ducked out back doors and taken roundabout ways through campus. She was, I don't know, scarce.

I found myself looking at her in class. The teacher'd be talking and all eyes would be up front . . . except mine. They kept wandering over to Juli. It was weird. One minute I'd be listening to the teacher, and the next I'd be completely tuned out, looking at Juli.

It wasn't until Wednesday in math that I figured it out. With the way her hair fell back over her shoulders

123

and her head was tilted, she looked like the picture in the paper. Not just like it—the angle was different, and the wind wasn't blowing through her hair—but she did look like the picture. A lot like the picture.

Making that connection sent a chill down my spine. And I wondered—what was she thinking? Could she really be that interested in root derivations?

Darla Tressler caught me watching, and man, she gave me the world's wickedest smile. If I didn't do something fast, this was going to spread like wildfire, so I squinted at her and whispered, "There's a bee in her hair, stupid," then pointed around in the air like, There it goes, see?

Darla's neck whipped around searching for the bee, and I straightened out my focus for the rest of the day. The last thing I needed was to be scorched by the likes of Darla Tressler.

That night I was doing my homework, and just to prove to myself that I'd been wrong, I pulled that news-paper article out of my trash can. And as I'm flipping it over, I'm telling myself, It's a distortion of reality; it's my imagination; she doesn't really look like that. . . .

But there she was. The girl in my math class, two rows over and one seat up, glowing through newsprint.

Lynetta barged in. "I need your sharpener," she said.

I slammed my binder closed over the paper and said, "You're supposed to knock!" And then, since she was zooming in and the paper was still sticking out, I crammed the binder into my backpack as fast as I could.

"What are you trying to hide there, baby brother?"

"Nothing, and stop calling me that! And don't barge into my room anymore!"

"Give me your sharpener and I'm history," she said with her hand out.

I dug it out of my drawer and tossed it at her, and sure enough, she disappeared.

But two seconds later my mom was calling for me, and after that, well, I forgot that the paper was in my binder.

Until first period the next morning, that is. Man! What was I supposed to do with it? I couldn't get up and throw it out; Garrett was right there. Besides that, Darla Tressler's in that class, and I could tell—she was keeping an eye out for wayward bees. If she caught wind of this, I'd be the one stung.

Then Garrett reaches over to snag a piece of paper like he does about fourteen times a day, only I have a complete mental spaz and slam down on his hand with mine.

"Dude!" he says. "What's your problem?"

"Sorry," I say, tuning in to the fact that he was only going for lined paper, not newspaper.

"Dude," he says again. "You know you've been really spaced lately? Anyone else tell you that?" He rips a piece of paper out of my binder, then notices the edges of the newspaper. He eyes me, and before I can stop him, he whips it out.

I pounce on him and tear it out of his hands, but it's too late. He's seen her picture.

Before he can say a word, I get in his face and say, "You shut up, you hear me? This is not what you think."

"Whoa, kick back, will ya? I wasn't thinking any-thing. . . ." But I could see the little gears go *click-click-*

click in his brain. Then he smirks at me and says, "I'm sure you've got a perfectly reasonable explanation for why you're carrying a picture of Juli Baker around with you."

The way he said it scared me. Like he was playing with the idea of roasting me in front of the whole class. I leaned over and said, "Zip it, would you?"

The teacher hammered on us to be quiet, but it didn't stop Garrett from smirking at me or doing the double-eyebrow wiggle in the direction of my binder. After class Darla tried to act all cool and preoccupied, but she had her radar up and pointed our way. She shadowed me practically all day, so there was no real window of opportunity to explain things to Garrett.

126

What was I going to tell him, anyway? That the paper was in my binder because I was trying to hide it from my sister? *That* would help.

Besides, I didn't want to make up some lame lie about it. I actually *wanted* to talk to Garrett. I mean, he was my friend, and a lot had happened in the last couple of months that was weighing on me. I thought that if I talked to him, maybe he'd help get me back on track. Help me to stop thinking about everything. Garrett was real reliable in that arena.

Luckily, in social studies our class got library time to do research for our famous historical figure report. Darla and Juli were both in that class, but I managed to drag Garrett into a back corner of the library without either of them noticing. And the minute we were by ourselves, I found myself laying into Garrett about chickens.

He shakes his head at me and says, "Dude! What are you *talking* about?"

"Remember when we went and looked over her fence?"

"Back in the sixth grade?"

"Yeah. Remember how you were down on me for wondering what a hen was?"

He rolled his eyes. "Not this again...."

"Man, you didn't know jack-diddly-squat about chickens. I put my life in your hands and you dumped me in a bucket of bull."

So I told him about my dad and the eggs and salmonella and how I'd been intercepting eggs for nearly two years.

He just shrugged and said, "Makes sense to me."

"Man, she caught me!"

"Who?"

"Juli!"

"Whoa, dude!"

127

I told him about what I'd said, and how almost right after that she was out playing weed warrior in her front yard.

"Well, so? It's not your fault her yard's a mess."

"But then I found out that they don't even own that house. They're all poor because her dad's got a retarded brother that they're, you know, paying for."

Garrett gives me a real chumpy grin and says, "A retard? Well, that explains a lot, doesn't it?"

I couldn't believe my ears. "What?"

"You know," he says, still grinning, "about Juli."

My heart started pounding and my hands clenched up. And for the first time since I'd learned to dive away from trouble, I wanted to deck somebody.

But we were in the *library*. And besides, it flashed

through my mind that if I decked him for what he'd said, he'd turn around and tell everyone that I was hot for Juli Baker, and I was not hot for Juli Baker!

So I made myself laugh and say, "Oh, right," and then came up with an excuse to put some *distance* between him and me.

After school Garrett asked me to come to his house and hang for a while, but I had zero interest in that. I still wanted to slug him.

I tried to talk myself down from feeling that way, but in my gut I was flaming mad at the guy. He'd crossed the line, man. He'd crossed it big-time.

And what made the whole thing so stinking hard to ignore was the fact that standing right next to him, on the other side of the line, was my father.

128

The Visit

Sunday mornings are peaceful in our house. My father lets himself sleep in. My mother lets herself not fix breakfast. And if my brothers have been out late playing with their band, you won't even know they're around until noon.

Usually I tiptoe out to collect eggs while everyone else is asleep, then spirit a bowl of Cheerios back to my room to have breakfast in bed and read.

But that Sunday—after spending most of the night feeling upset or uneasy—I woke up wanting to do something physical. To shake off the confused way I was still feeling.

What I really needed was a good climb in my sycamore tree, but I settled for watering the lawn while I tried to think of other things. I cranked open the spigot and admired how rich and black the dirt looked as I sprinkled back and forth across the soil. And I was busy talking to my buried seedlings, coaxing them to spring up and greet the rising sun, when my father came outside. His hair was damp from a shower, and he had a grocery sack rolled closed in his hand. "Dad! I'm sorry if I woke you."

"You didn't, sweetheart. I've been up for a while."

"You're not going to work, are you?"

"No, I..." He studied me for a moment, then said, "I'm going to visit David."

"*Uncle* David?"

He walked toward his truck, saying, "That's right. I...I should be back around noon."

"But Dad, why today? It's Sunday."

"I know, sweetheart, but it's a special Sunday."

I turned off the spigot. "Why's that?"

"It's his fortieth birthday. I want to see him and deliver a gift," he said as he held up the paper bag. "Don't worry. I'll rustle us up some pancakes for lunch, all right?"

"I'm coming with you," I said, and tossed the hose aside. I wasn't even really dressed—I'd just pulled on some sweats and sneakers, no socks—but in my mind there was no doubt. I was going.

"Why don't you stay home and enjoy the morning with your mother? I'm sure she would—"

I went over to the passenger side of his truck and said, "I'm coming," then climbed inside and slammed the door back in place.

"But—" he said through the driver's door.

"I'm coming, Dad."

He studied me a moment, then said, "Okay," and put the bag on the bench seat. "Let me leave a note for your mother."

While he was inside, I strapped on the lap belt and told myself that this was good. This was something I should've done years ago. Uncle David was part of the family, part of my father, part of me. It was about time I got to know him.

I studied the paper sack sitting next to me. What was my father bringing his brother for his fortieth birthday?

130

I picked it up. It wasn't a painting—it was much too light for that. Plus, it made a strange, muted rattling noise when I shook it.

I was just unrolling the top to peek inside when my father came back through the front door. I dropped the sack and straightened up, and when he slid behind the wheel, I said, "It's okay with you, isn't it?"

He just looked at me, his hand on the key in the ignition.

"I . . . I'm not ruining your day with him or anything, am I?"

He cranked the motor and said, "No, sweetheart. I'm glad you're coming."

We didn't say much to each other on the drive over to Greenhaven. He seemed to want to look at the scenery and I, well, I had a lot of questions, but none I wanted to ask. It was nice, though, riding with my father. It was like the silence connected us in a way that explanations never could.

When we arrived at Greenhaven, my father parked the truck, but we didn't get out right away. "It takes some getting used to, Julianna, but it does grow on you. *They* grow on you. They're all good people."

I nodded, but felt oddly afraid.

"Come on, then," he said, taking the sack from the seat. "Let's go inside."

Greenhaven didn't look like any kind of hospital to me, but it didn't look quite like a house, either. It was too long and rectangular for that. The walkway had a faded green awning that covered it, and flower beds alongside with freshly planted pansies that looked muddied and slightly askew. The grass was patchy, with three deep holes dug near the building.

"The residents tend the grounds," my father said. "It's part of their occupational training program, and it's therapeutic. Those holes are the future homes of Peach, Plum, and Pear."

"Fruit trees?"

"Yes. The vote caused quite a commotion."

"Among the...residents?"

"That's right." He swung open one of the glass double doors and said, "Come on in."

It was cool inside. And it smelled of pine cleaner and bleach, with something vaguely pungent underneath.

There wasn't a reception desk or waiting area, just a large intersection with white walls and narrow wooden benches. To the left was a big room with a television and several rows of plastic chairs, to the right were open office doors, and beside us were two pine armoires. One was open, with half a dozen gray sweaters hung neatly in a row.

"Good morning, Robert!" a woman called through one of the office doors.

"Good morning, Josie," my father replied.

She came out to meet us, saying, "David's up and about. Has been since around six. Mabel tells me it's his birthday today."

"Mabel is right again." He turned to me and smiled. "Josie, it's my pleasure to introduce my daughter, Julianna. Julianna, meet Josie Gruenmakker."

"Well now, isn't this nice," Josie said, clasping my hand. "I recognize you from David's photo album. You're gettin' ready to graduate into high school, isn't that right?"

I blinked at her, then looked at my dad. I'd never really thought of it that way, but I could see that he had. "Yes, I...I suppose I am."

132

"Josie's the site administrator."

"And," Josie added with a laugh, "I'm not graduatin' to nowhere! Been here seventeen years, and I'm staying put." The phone rang and she hurried off, saying, "Gotta get that. I'll meet up with you in a bit. Check the rec room, then his room. You'll find him."

My dad led me around a corner, and as we proceeded down a hallway, the underlying pungent part of the smell got stronger. Like the place had had years of Mystery Pissers, with no one quite neutralizing what had been tagged.

Down the hall was a small person hunched in a wheelchair. At first I thought it was a child, but as we approached, I could see it was a woman. She had almost no hair, and as she gave my dad a toothless smile, she grabbed his hand and spoke.

My heart bottomed out. The sounds she made were choked and lost on her tongue. Nothing she said was intelligible, yet she looked at my father with such intensity — like of course he understood what she was saying.

To my complete surprise, he said, "You're absolutely right, Mabel. It is today. Which is why I'm here." He held up the grocery sack and whispered, "I've brought him a little gift."

"Gwa-aaal," she said.

"How'd you know?"

She gurgled at him until he patted her hand and said, "I'm much too predictable, I'm afraid. But he enjoys them, and..." He noticed her gaze shift in my direction.

"Hoo haa," she said.

"This is my daughter, Julianna. Julianna, I'd like you to meet the extraordinary Miss Mabel. She can remember

133

everyone's birthday, and she has a real passion for strawberry milkshakes."

I managed a smile and whispered, "Nice to meet you," but all I got in return was a suspicious scowl.

"Well, we're off to David's," my father said, then shook the bag. "Don't spill the beans if he happens by."

I followed him to a bedroom doorway, where he stopped and called, "David? David, it's Robert."

A man appeared at the door. A man I would never have picked out as my father's brother. He was stocky, with thick brown glasses, and his face looked puffy and pale. But he threw his arms around my father's chest and cried, "Wobbad! Yaw heew!"

"Yes, I am, little brother."

134   I followed them into the room and saw that the walls were covered in a collage of puzzles. They'd been glued directly to the walls and even up on the ceiling! It was cozy and comfortable, and interesting. I felt as though I'd entered a quilted cave.

My father held his brother at arm's length and said, "And look who I've brought along!"

For a split second David looked almost frightened, but then my father said, "It's my daughter, Julianna."

David's face broke into a smile. "Ju-weee-an-na!" he cried, then practically tackled me with a hug.

I thought I was going to suffocate. My face was buried as he squeezed the air out of me and rocked from side to side. Then with a giggle he let go and flopped into a chair. "Is mooy bwuf-day!"

"I know, Uncle David. Happy birthday!"

He giggled again. "Fwank eoow!"

J U L I A N N A

"We brought you a present," my dad said as he opened the paper sack.

Before he had it out, before I saw the actual size, I remembered the sound it had made when I'd shaken it in the truck. Of course! I thought. A puzzle.

Uncle David guessed it, too. "A puwwwle?"

"Not just a puzzle," my dad said as he pulled it out of the sack. "A puzzle and a pinwheel."

Dad had wrapped the puzzle box up in pretty blue paper and had taped the red-and-yellow pinwheel on as a bow. Uncle David snatched the pinwheel right off and blew. First gently, then fiercely, in great spitty bursts. "Ownge!" he cried between blows. "Ownge!"

Very gently Dad took it from him and smiled. "Red and yellow do make orange, don't they?" David tried to grab it back, but my father said, "We'll take it outside later. The wind will blow it for you," and pressed the puzzle back in his hands.

As the wrapping paper fell in shreds on the floor, I leaned in to see what sort of puzzle my father had bought him and gasped. Three thousand pieces! And the image was simply white clouds and blue sky. No shading, no trees—nothing but the clouds and the sky.

My father pointed to a spot in the center of the ceiling. "I thought it would fit just right over there."

Uncle David looked up and nodded, then lunged for his pinwheel and said, "Owsiiide?"

"Sure. Let's go out for a walk. Feel like going down to McElliot's for a birthday ice cream?"

Uncle David's head bobbed up and down. "Yaaah!"

We checked out through Josie, then headed down the

street. David can't walk very fast because his body seems to want to move inward instead of forward. His feet pigeon-toe and his shoulders hunch in, and he seemed to lean on my father pretty heavily as we moved along.

But he kept that pinwheel in front of him, watching it spin, crying every now and then, "Owwwange, owwwange!"

McElliot's turned out to be a drugstore with an ice cream parlor inside. There was a red-and-white-striped awning over the ice cream counter, and there were little white tables and chairs set in an area with red-and-white-striped wallpaper. It was very festive-looking, especially for being inside a drugstore.

Dad got us all cones, and once we were sitting down, Dad and David did talk to each other some, but mostly David wanted to eat his chocolate fudge swirl. My father smiled at me from time to time, and I smiled back, but I felt disconnected. How many times had the two of them come here for ice cream? How many birthdays had my father celebrated with his brother like this? How long had he known Mabel and Josie and the rest of the people at Greenhaven? How could it be that in all these years, I'd never spent any time with my uncle? It was like my father had a secret life away from me. A complete *family* away from me.

I didn't like it. Didn't understand it. And I was getting myself pretty worked up about it when David's cone crushed in his grip, causing his ice cream to flop onto the table.

Before my dad could stop him, David picked up the ice cream and tried to cram it back onto the cone. But the cone was shattered and the ice cream fell over again, only this time it landed on the floor.

136

JULIANNA

My dad said, "Leave it, David. I'll get you a new one," but David didn't listen. His chair shot back and he dove after it.

"No, David! Let me get you a new one." My dad pulled him by the arm, but David wouldn't budge. He grabbed the ice cream and crammed it back onto what was left of his cone, and when the bottom part of his cone crumbled completely away, he started screaming.

It was awful. He was like a two-hundred-pound infant, throwing a tantrum on the floor. He was yelling words I couldn't understand, and after a minute of trying to calm him down, my father said, "Julianna, can you get him another cone?"

The man behind the counter scooped as fast as he could, but in that short time David knocked over a table and two chairs with his flailing and managed to smear chocolate everywhere. The checkers and customers at the registers seemed frozen with terror—like David was some sort of monster out to destroy the world.

I gave the new cone to my father, who handed it to David, right there on the floor. And while David sat there eating it, my father and I worked around him, putting everything back in order and wiping up the mess.

On the walk back to Greenhaven, David acted like nothing had happened. He spurted into his pinwheel and cried, "Owwwange!" from time to time, but when my dad held open the front door, I could tell that David was tired.

Down in his room David placed the pinwheel on his bed and picked up the puzzle box. "Why don't you take a rest before you get started on it?" my dad asked.

David shook his head. "Naaow."

"Okay, then. Let me help you set it up."

My father pulled a card table from beneath the bed, then swung the legs out and snapped them into place. After he had it shoved up against the wall near the bed, he moved a chair close to it and said, "There you are. All set up."

David had the box open and was already sifting through the pieces. "Aaaas a gou wwwone, Wobbad."

"I'm glad you like it. You think you might have it done by Wednesday? I can come back and glue it on the ceiling for you then if you'd like."

David nodded, but he was already intent on the puzzle, carefully laying pieces on the table. My father put his hand on his shoulder and said, "I'll see you Wednesday then, okay?"

He nodded.

"Will you say good-bye to Julianna?"

"Baaawye," he said, but he didn't look up from his box of pieces.

"See you later, Uncle David." I tried to sound cheerful, but I didn't feel that way.

When we got back into the truck, my dad clicked on his seat belt and said, "So."

I just looked at him and tried to smile.

"Are you as exhausted as I am?" he said.

I nodded. "Everything was fine—except for the ice cream."

Dad chuckled. "Except for the ice cream." Then he turned serious. "The trouble is, you never know what 'the ice cream' is going to be. Sometimes it's a fly in the room. Sometimes it's the feel of his socks. It's hard to predict every-thing. Usually getting ice cream is safe." He shook his head

138

JULIANNA

and closed his eyes, thinking things I couldn't imagine. Finally he turned the ignition and said, "David lived with your mother and me for a while. Before you kids were born. We thought it would be better for him to live with us than to be in a home, but we were wrong."

"But overall, everything went okay today...."

He ground the gearshift into reverse. "David has many, *many* special needs, both emotional and physical. Your mom and I couldn't handle them all. Fortunately he's happy here. They have programs to teach him how to care for himself— how to dress and bathe and brush his teeth, how to act around others and communicate. They go on outings, and he has a job doing mailings for a doctor's office...."

"He does?"

"He goes there every morning during the week to fold mailings and fill envelopes. Greenhaven's been so good for him. He gets an incredible amount of individualized attention. He has his own room, his own friends, his own life."

After a minute I said, "But he's part of the family, Dad. And it just doesn't seem right that he's never been over for a visit. Not even on Christmas or Thanksgiving!"

"He doesn't want to, sweetheart. One year your mother and I insisted he spend Thanksgiving with us, and it was the biggest disaster you can imagine. He broke a window out of the car, he was that upset."

"But...why haven't we been visiting *him?* I know you have, but the rest of us. Why not?"

"Well, it's draining. Your mother finds it incredibly depressing, and I understand that. We both agreed that it was no place to take small children." He accelerated onto the highway, silent behind the wheel. Finally he said, "The years just seem to slip away, Julianna. One day you have a baby in your arms, and the next you realize she's very nearly a woman." He smiled at me sadly. "I love David, but he is a burden, and I guess I wanted to protect you from that. But I realize now that all of this *has* affected you and the family."

"But Dad, it's not—"

"Julianna, what I'm trying to tell you is I'm sorry. There was so much I wanted to give you. All of you. I guess I didn't see until recently how little I've actually provided."

"That's not true!"

"Well, I think you know my heart's been in the right place, but if you line it up objectively, a man like, say, Mr. Loski adds up to a much better husband and father than a man like me does. He's around more, he provides more, and he's probably a lot more fun."

My dad wasn't one to go fishing for compliments or signs of appreciation, but still, I couldn't quite believe he actually *thought* that. "Dad, I don't care how it looks on paper, I think you're the best dad ever! And when I marry somebody someday, I sure don't want him to be like Mr. Loski! I want him to be like you."

He looked at me like he couldn't quite believe *his* ears. "Is that so," he said with a grin. "Well, I'll remind you of that as your someday approaches."

That turned the rest of the trip around. We laughed and joked and talked about all kinds of things, but as we neared home, there was one thing the conversation kept turning back to.

Pancakes.

140

My mother, though, had other plans. She'd spent the morning scrubbing floors and nixed the pancakes. "I need something with more staying power. Like grilled ham-and-cheese. With onions," she said. "Lots of onions!"

"Scrubbing floors?" my dad said. "It's Sunday, Trina. Why were you scrubbing floors?"

"Nervous energy." She looked at me. "How'd it go?"

"Okay. I'm glad I went."

She glanced at my dad and then at me. "Well, good," she sighed, then said, "I also felt like scrubbing because I got a call from Patsy."

"Loski?" my dad asked. "Is something wrong?"

My mother pushed a few wisps of hair back and said, "No....She called to invite us over for dinner on Friday."

We blinked at her a moment; then I asked, "All of us?"

"Yes."

141

I could see what my dad was thinking: Why? All these years of living across the street, and we'd never been invited over. Why now?

My mom could see it, too. She sighed and said, "Robert, I don't exactly know why, but she was insistent. She was practically in tears, saying how sorry she was that she'd never invited us before and how she'd really like to get to know us better."

"What did you tell her?"

"I couldn't very well say no. She was being so nice, and Chet has really done a lot...." She shrugged and said, "I said we'd go. It's set for six o'clock Friday night."

"Really?" I asked.

She shrugged again. "I think it might be nice. A little strange, but nice."

JULIANNA

"Well, okay then," my dad said. "I won't schedule any overtime for Friday. What about the boys?"

"There's no gig on the calendar, and they're not scheduled to work, but I haven't talked to them about it yet."

"Are you sure they want us *all* over there?" my dad asked.

My mom nodded. "She insists."

I could tell the whole idea of dinner at the Loskis' was making my dad pretty uncomfortable, but we could both see that something about this invitation meant a lot to my mother. "All right then," he said, and got to work slicing cheese and onions.

For the rest of the afternoon, I sort of lazed around, reading and daydreaming. And at school the next day, I couldn't seem to concentrate. My thoughts kept turning back to David. I wondered what my grandparents had been like, and what they'd gone through, having a son like him.

142

I daydreamed a lot about the sycamore tree, too, which at first I thought was because I was feeling melancholy. But then I remembered how my mother had called the sycamore a testimony to endurance. It had survived being damaged as a sapling. It had grown. Other people thought it was ugly, but I never had.

Maybe it was all how you looked at it. Maybe there were things I saw as ugly that other people thought were beautiful.

Like Shelly Stalls. A perfect example! To me there was absolutely nothing to recommend her, but the rest of the world seemed to think she was the cat's meow.

Me-ow.

Anyway, I sort of drifted through the week like that. Until Thursday. Thursday our social studies class went to the library to do research for our famous historical figure report. I'd chosen Susan B. Anthony and her fight for the right to vote, and I was in the middle of tracking down some books when Darla Tressler flagged me from the end of a stack.

Darla was in a few of my classes, but we weren't really friends, so I looked behind me to see who else she might be flagging.

"Come here!" she mouthed, frantically waving me over.

So I hurried over. She pointed through the column of books and whispered, "Listen!"

It was Garrett's voice. And then Bryce's. And they were talking about...me. About my chickens. And salmonella poisoning. And how Bryce had been throwing away my eggs. And about me fixing up our yard.

Bryce was sounding like he felt really bad, but then suddenly my blood ran cold. He was talking about David!

And then Garrett laughed and said, "A retard? Well, that explains a lot, doesn't it? You know...about Juli?"

For a second, there was silence. And at that moment I was sure they must be able to hear my heart pounding in my chest, but then Bryce laughed and said, "Oh, right."

I positively crumbled onto the floor. And in a flash the voices were gone. Darla checked around the corner, then sat beside me, saying, "Oh, Jules, I'm so, so sorry. I thought he was about to confess that he's been crushing on you."

"What? Darla, Bryce does not have a crush on me."

"Where have you been? Haven't you noticed the way he's been looking at you? That boy is lost in Loveland."

"Oh, obviously! You just heard him, Darla!"

"Yeah, but yesterday, yesterday I caught him staring at you and he said there was a bee in your hair. A bee, girl. Is that the lamest cover-up you've ever heard or what?"

"Darla, the way things have been going, I wouldn't be surprised if there *was* a bee in my hair."

"Oh, you think you're that sweet, huh? Just attract bees like honey? Well, honey, the only bee you're attracting around here is B-r-y-c-e. Cute, yeah. But after what I just heard, I'd stomp and grind, girl. Stomp and grind." She got up to go but turned and said, "Don't worry. I won't jabber."

I just shook my head and forgot about Darla. How wrong could a person be.

It was what Bryce and Garrett had said that I couldn't forget. How could they be so cruel? And so stupid? Is this what my father had gone through growing up?

The more I thought about it, the angrier I got. What right did Bryce have to make fun of my uncle? How dare he!

I felt fire burn in my cheeks and a cold, hard knot tighten in my heart. And in a flash I knew—I was *through* with Bryce Loski. He could keep his brilliant blue eyes. He could keep his two-faced smile and...and my kiss. That's right! He could keep that, too. I was never, ever going to talk to him again!

I stormed back to the section of books on Susan B. Anthony, found two that would work, and then went back to my table. But as I was collecting my things to check out of the library, I remembered. The next day we were going to the Loskis' house for dinner.

I zipped up my backpack and threw it on my shoulder. Surely after what had happened, I had the right to vote against going!

Didn't I?

J U L I A N N A

The Serious Willies

Realizing that my father had the same sense of humor as *Garrett* gave me the serious willies. I had the hardest time just looking at my dad, let alone speaking to him. But at about five o'clock Friday afternoon I agreed with him about one thing—we should've barbecued. A barbecue is more, you know, low-key. Instead, my mom was flying around the kitchen, slicing and dicing and barking orders at Dad and me like the president was coming to dinner.

145

We swept the floor, put an extra leaf in the table, brought in five more chairs, and set the table. We set it all wrong, of course, but all my mother had to do was shuffle things around to make it right. It looked the same to me, but what do I know?

She put out candlesticks and said, "Rick, can you load the dishes and run them? I'd like a chance to get cleaned up. After that you can change. And Bryce? What are you wearing?"

"Mom, it's the *Bakers*. Are you trying to make them feel totally worthless?"

"Trina and I agreed on a dress-up, so—"

"But why?"

My dad put a hand on my shoulder and said, "So we can all feel equally uncomfortable, son."

Women. I looked at her and said, "Does that mean I have to wear a *tie*?"

"No, but some sort of button-down instead of a T-shirt would be nice."

I went down to my room and ripped through my closet looking for something with buttons. There were lots of buttons, all right. Lots of geeky buttons. I thought about boycotting my mother's dress-code requirements, but instead I started putting on shirts.

Twenty minutes later I still wasn't dressed. And I was extremely ticked off about it because what did it matter? Why did I care what I looked like at this stupid dinner? I was acting like a girl.

Then through a gap in my curtains I saw them coming. Out their front door, down their walkway, across the street. It was like a weird dream. They seemed to be floating toward our house. All five of them.

I pulled a shirt off my bed, punched my arms in, and buttoned up.

Two seconds later the doorbell rang and Mom called, "Can you get that, Bryce?"

Luckily, Granddad beat me to it. He greeted them all like they were long-lost family and even seemed to know which one was Matt and which one was Mike. One was wearing a purple shirt and the other was wearing a green one, so it shouldn't have been that hard to remember which was which, but they came in and pinched my cheeks and said, "Hey, baby brother! How's it goin'?" and I got so mad I mixed them up again.

My mother zoomed in from the kitchen, saying, "Come in, come *in*. It's so nice you all could make it." She called,

146

"Lyn-et-ta! Rick! We've got com-pa-ny!" but then stopped short when she saw Juli and Mrs. Baker. "Well, what's this?" she asked. "Homemade pies?"

Mrs. Baker said, "Blackberry cheesecake and pecan."

"They look wonderful! Absolutely wonderful!" My mother was acting so hyper I couldn't believe it. She took Juli's pie, then whooshed a path to the kitchen with Mrs. Baker.

Lynetta appeared from around the corner, which made Matt and Mike grin and say, "Hey, Lyn. Lookin' good."

Black skirt, black nails, black eyes—for a nocturnal rodent, yeah, I suppose she was looking good.

They disappeared down to Lynetta's room, and when I turned around, my granddad was taking Mr. Baker into the front room, which left me in the entry hall with Juli. Alone.

She wasn't looking at me. She seemed to be looking at everything *but* me. And I felt like an idiot, standing there in my geeky button-down shirt with pinched cheeks and nothing to say. And I got so nervous about having nothing to say that my heart started going wacko on me, hammering like it does right before a race or a game or something.

On top of that, she looked more like that stupid picture in the paper than the picture did, if that makes any sense. Not because she was all dressed up—she wasn't. She was wearing some normal-looking dress and normal-looking shoes, and her hair was the way it always is except maybe a little more brushed out. It was the way she was looking at everything but me, with her shoulders back and her chin out and her eyes flashing.

We probably only stood there for five seconds, but it felt like a year. Finally I said, "Hi, Juli."

Her eyes flashed at me, and that's when it sank in—she was mad. She whispered, "I heard you and Garrett making fun of my uncle in the library, and I don't want to speak to you! You understand me? Not now, not ever!"

My mind was racing. Where had she been? I hadn't seen her anywhere near me in the library! And had *she* heard it? Or had she heard it from somebody else.

I tried to tell her it wasn't me, that it was Garrett, all Garrett. But she shut me down and made tracks for the front room to be with her dad.

So I'm standing there, wishing I'd punched Garrett out in the library so Juli wouldn't stick me in the same class as someone who makes *retard* jokes, when my dad shows up and claps me on the shoulder. "So. How's the party, son?"

Speak of the devil. I wanted to whack his hand off my shoulder.

He leans out so he can see into the front room and says, "Hey, the dad cleans up pretty good, doesn't he?"

I shrug away from him. "Mr. Baker's name is Robert, Dad."

"Yeah, you know, I knew that." He rubs his hands together and says, "I guess I ought to go in and say hello. Coming?"

"Nah. Mom probably needs my help."

I didn't run off to the kitchen, though. I stood there and watched Mr. Baker shake my father's hand. And as they stood there pumping and smiling, this weird feeling started coming over me again. Not about Juli—about my father. Standing next to Mr. Baker, he looked small. Physically small. And compared to the cut of Mr. Baker's jaw, my dad's face looked kind of weaselly.

This is not the way you want to feel about your father. When I was little, I'd always thought that my dad was right about everything and that there wasn't a man on earth he couldn't take. But standing there looking in, I realized that Mr. Baker could squash him like a bug.

Worse, though, was the way he was acting. Watching my dad chum it up with Juli's dad—it was like seeing him lie. To Mr. Baker, to Juli, to my grandfather—to everybody. Why was he being such a worm? Why couldn't he just act normal? You know, civil? Why did he have to put on such a phony show? This went way beyond keeping the peace with my mother. This was disgusting.

149

And people said I was the spitting image of my father. How often had I heard that one? I'd never thought about it much, but now it was turning my stomach.

Mom jingled the dinner bell and called, "Hors d'oeuvres are ready!" and then saw me still standing in the hallway. "Bryce, where'd your sister and the boys go?"

I shrugged. "Down to her room, I think."

"Go tell them, would you? And then come have some hors d'oeuvres."

"Sure," I said. Anything to get rid of the taste in my mouth.

Lynetta's door was closed. And normally I would have knocked and called, Mom wants you, or, Dinner! or something, but in that split second before my knuckles hit wood, my hand became possessed by Evil Baby Brother. I turned the knob and walked right in.

Does Lynetta freak out or throw stuff at me and scream for me to get out? No. She ignores me. Matt-and-Mike give me a nod, and Lynetta sees me, but she's got her hands over some headphones and her whole body's bobbing up and down as she listens to a portable CD player.

Matt-or-Mike whispers, "It's about over. We'll be right there," like of course I was there to say it was time to eat. What else would I be doing there?

Something about that made me feel, I don't know, left out. I wasn't even a person to those guys. I was just baby brother.

Nothing new there, but now it really bugged me. Like all of a sudden I didn't fit in anywhere. Not at school, not at home . . . and every time I turned around, another person I'd known forever felt like a stranger to me. Even *I* felt like a stranger to me.

Standing around eating little round crackers smeared with whipped cheese and fish eggs didn't do much for my mood either. My mother was acting like an entire swarm of busy bees. She was everywhere. In the kitchen, out of the kitchen. Serving drinks, handing out napkins. Explaining the food, but not eating a thing.

Lynetta didn't buy Mom's explanation on the hors d'oeuvres—she wound up dissecting hers, categorizing the parts into gross, disgusting, and revolting.

Hanging near her didn't stop the Baker boys from shoving crackers in whole, though. Man, I was just waiting for them to wrap themselves around a table leg and flex.

Juli, her dad, and my grandfather were off to the side

talking nonstop about something, and my dad was over
with Mrs. Baker looking about as stupid as I felt, standing by myself talking to no one.

My mom flutters over to me and says, "You doing
okay, honey?"

"Yeah," I tell her, but she forces me over to where
Granddad is anyway. "Go on, go on," she whispers.
"Dinner will be ready in a minute."

So I stand there and the group of them opens up, but
it's more like a reflex than anything. No one says a word
to me. They just keep right on talking about perpetual
motion.

Perpetual motion.

My friend, I didn't even know what perpetual motion
was. They were talking closed systems, open systems,
resistance, energy source, magnetism . . . it was like join-
ing a discussion in a different language. And Juli, *Juli*
was saying stuff like, "Well, what if you put the magnets
back to back—reversed the polarity?" like she really
understood what they were talking about. Then my
granddad and her dad would explain why her idea
wouldn't work, but all that did was make Juli ask
another question.

I was completely lost. And even though I was pretending to follow along with what they were saying, what
I was really doing was trying not to stare at Juli.

When my mom called us for dinner, I did my best to
pull Juli aside and apologize to her, but she gave me the
cold shoulder, and who could blame her, really?

I sat down across from her, feeling pretty low. Why
hadn't I said something to Garrett in the library? I didn't

have to punch him. Why hadn't I just told him he was out of line?

After Mom served everyone their food, Dad seemed to decide that he ought to be the one directing the conversation. "So, Mike and Matt," he says, "you're seniors this year."

"Amen!" they say together.

"Amen? As in you're glad high school's over?"

"Absolutely."

My father starts twirling his fork. "Why's that?"

Matt and Mike look at each other, then back at my dad. "The regurgitation gets to you after a while."

"Isn't that funny," he says, looking around the table. "High school was probably the best time of my life."

Matt-or-Mike says, "Seriously? Dude, it's totally lame!" Mrs. Baker shoots him a look, but that doesn't stop him. "Well, it is, Mom. It's that whole robotron attitude of education. Confine, confute, conform—I've had totally enough of that scene."

My dad eyes my mom with a little I-told-you-so grin, then says to Matt and Mike, "So I take it college is out of the question?"

God, what was *with* him? In a flash I was clutching my fork and knife, ready to duke it out for a couple of guys who pinched my cheeks and called me baby brother.

I took a deep breath and tried to relax. Tried to dive down to calmer water. This wasn't my fight.

Besides, Matt and Mike seemed cool with it. "Oh, no," they said. "College is a total possibility." "Yeah, we got accepted a couple of places, but we're going to give the music thing a shot first."

152

"Oh, the *music* thing," my father says.

Matt and Mike look at each other, then shrug and get back to eating. But Lynetta glares at him and says, "Your sarcasm is not appreciated, Dad."

"Lyn, Lyn," says Matt-or-Mike. "It's cool. Everyone's like that about it. It's a show-me-don't-tell-me thing."

"That's a great idea," Lynetta says, jumping out of her seat and dashing down the hall.

Mom freezes, not sure what to do about Lynetta, but then Mrs. Baker says, "Dinner is absolutely delicious, Patsy."

"Thanks, Trina. It's . . . it's nice to have all of you over."

There's about three seconds of quiet and then Lynetta comes in and jabs at the CD player buttons until the drawer slides back in.

153

"Lyn, no! Not a good idea," says Matt-or-Mike. "Yeah, Lyn. It's not exactly dinner music."

"Tough," says Lynetta, and cranks the volume.

Boom, whack! Boom-boom, whack! The candles practically shake in their holders; then guitars rip through the air and about blow them out. Matt and Mike look up at the speakers, then grin at each other and call over to my dad, "Surround sound—awesome setup, Mr. Loski!"

All the adults were dying to jump up and turn the thing down, but Lynetta stood guard and just glowered at them. And when the song's over, Lynetta pulls out the CD, punches off the player, and then smiles— actually smiles—at Matt and Mike and says, "That is the raddest song. I want to hear it again and again and again."

Matt-or-Mike says to my dad, "You probably don't like it, but it's what we do."

"You boys wrote that song?"

"Uh-huh."

He motions Lynetta to pass the CD over, saying, "Just the one song?"

Matt-or-Mike laughs and says, "Dude, we've got a thousand songs, but there's only three on the demo."

Dad holds up the CD. "This is the demo?"

"Yeah."

He looks at it a minute and says, "So if you're Piss Poor, how do you afford to press CDs?"

"Dad!" Lynetta snaps at him.

154   "It's okay, Lyn. Just a joke, right, Mr. Loski?"

My dad laughs a little and says, "Right," but then adds, "Although I am a little curious. This is obviously not a home-done demo, and I happen to know studio time's cost-prohibitive for most bands...."

Matt and Mike interrupt him with a slamming hard high five. And while I'm getting uptight about my dad asking them questions about money, of all things, my mom's fumbling all over herself, trying to sweep away my dad's big pawprints. "When Rick and I met, he was play-ing in a band...."

Poached salmon was suddenly swimming down the wrong hatch. And while I'm choking, Lynetta's bugging out her raccoon eyes, gasping, "*You?* Played in a *band*? What did you play, clarinet?"

"No, honey," my mom says, trying to hold it all together. "Your father played guitar."

"*Guitar?*"

"Cool!" Matt-or-Mike says. "Rock? Country? Jazz?"

"Country," my dad says. "Which is nothing to scoff at, boys."

"Dude! We know. Total respect, man."

"And when our band looked into getting a demo made, it was astronomically expensive. That was in a big city, where there was a little competition. Getting a demo made around here? I didn't even know there was a facility."

Matt and Mike are still grinning. "There's not."

"So where'd you go? And how'd you afford it?" My mother whacks him under the table again, so he says, "I'm just curious, Patsy!"

Matt and Mike lean in. "We did it ourselves."

155

"This right here? You did this yourselves? That's impossible." He's looking almost mad about it. "How'd you get the gear?"

My mom kicks him again, but Dad turns on her and says, "Stop it, would you? I'm just curious!"

Matt-or-Mike says, "It's cool, Mrs. Loski." He smiles at my dad and says, "We kept cruising the Internet and the trades looking for a deal. Everyone's blowing out their old analog gear for digital because that's the move everyone else has made. Digital, if you want to know our opinion, is *weak*. You lose too much of the waveform. There's not enough fat to it, and obviously we like it beefy."

My granddad puts up a finger and says, "But a CD's digital, so . . ."

"Exactly, but that is the last and *only* step we'll compromise on. It's just a necessity of being part of the industry. Everyone wants CDs. But the multitrack and the mixdown to two-track is analog. And we could afford it, Mr. Loski, because we got used gear and we've been saving up our pennies since we were twelve years old." He grins and says, "You still play? We could, you know, lay down some of your tunes if you want."

My dad looks down, and for a second I couldn't tell if he was going to get mad or cry. Then he sort of snorts and says, "Thanks, but that's not me anymore."

Which was probably the only honest thing my dad said all night. After that he was quiet. He'd try to plaster up a smile now and then, but man, underneath it he was broody. And I was feeling kind of bad for him. Was he thinking about the good old days playing in a band? I tried picturing him in cowboy boots and a cowboy hat, with a guitar strapped across his shoulder, playing some old Willie Nelson song.

He was right—it just wasn't him.

But the fact that it ever had been made me feel even more like a stranger in a strange land. Then, when the night was over and the Bakers were piling out the front door, something else strange happened. Juli touched my arm. And for the first time that night she was looking at me. It was *that* look, too, channeled directly and solely at me. She says, "I'm sorry I was so angry when we first came in. Everyone had a good time, and I think your mom's really nice for inviting us."

Her voice was quiet. Almost a whisper. I just stood there like a moron, staring at her.

"Bryce?" she says, touching my arm again. "Did you hear me? I'm sorry."

I managed a nod, but my arm was tingling, and my heart was pounding, and I felt myself pulling toward her.

Then she was gone. Out the door and into the night, part of a chorus of happy good-byes. I tried to catch my breath. What *was* that? What was wrong with me?

My mother closed the door and said, "There. Now what did I tell you? That is one delightful family! Those boys are nothing like I expected. Lynetta, why didn't you tell me they were so . . . so charming!"

"They're drug dealers is what they are."

Everyone turned to my father and dropped their jaws.

"What?" my mother said.

157

"There is no other way those boys could afford to buy recording gear like that." He glared at Lynetta. "Isn't that so?"

Lynetta's eyes looked like they were going to pop right out of her head.

"Rick, please!" my mother said. "You can't just make accusations like that!"

"It's the only thing that makes sense, Patsy. Believe me, I know how musicians are. There is no other explanation for this."

Lynetta shouted, "I happen to know for a fact that they don't use *or* deal. Where do you get off saying something like that? You are such a two-faced, condescending, narrow-minded jackass!"

There was a split second of silence, and then he slapped her, *smack,* right across the cheek.

That put my mother in his face like I'd never seen

and sent my sister screaming insults over her shoulder as she ran down to her room.

My heart was pounding. Lynetta was right and I almost, *almost* got in his face, too, and told him so. But then my granddad pulled me aside and we both retreated to our own little corners of the house.

Pacing around my room, I had the urge to go talk to Lynetta. To tell her that she was right, that Dad was way out of line. But I could hear her through the walls, crying and screaming while my mom tried to calm her down. Then she stormed out of the house to who-knows-where, and my mom took up with my dad again.

So I stayed put. And even though the earth quit quaking around eleven o'clock, there were tremors out there. I could feel them.

As I lay in my bed staring out the window at the sky, I thought about how my dad had always looked down on the Bakers. How he'd put down their house and their yard and their cars and what they did for a living. How he'd called them trash and made fun of Mr. Baker's paintings.

And now I was seeing that there was something really cool about that family. All of them. They were just...real.

And who were we? There was something spinning wickedly out of control inside this house. It was like seeing inside the Bakers' world had opened up windows into our own, and the view was not a pretty one.

Where had all this stuff come from?

And why hadn't I ever seen it before.

158

The Dinner

By the time I got home, I knew it would be selfish of me to boy-cott the Loskis' dinner party. My mother had already spent a lot of time humming over pie recipes and going through her closet for "something suitable to wear." She'd even bought a new shirt for Dad and had scrutinized what the boys intended to wear. Obviously she was looking forward to the dinner—not that I really understood that, but I didn't want to ruin everything by telling her about my newfound hatred of Bryce.

And Dad felt bad enough about David already. The last thing he needed was to hear about crackpot comments made by immature eighth graders.

So that night I went through the motions of baking pies with my mother and convinced myself that I was doing the right thing. One dinner couldn't change anyone's life. I just had to get through it.

Friday at school I avoided the blue-eyed brat the best I could, but that night as I got dressed, I found myself staring at the painting my father had given me and became furious all over again. Bryce had never been a friend to me, ever! He hadn't made a stand for the tree, he'd thrown away my eggs, and he'd made fun of me at my uncle's expense....Why was I playing along like we were jolly friends and neighbors?

When my mother called that it was time to go, I went out in the hall with every intention of telling her that I would not, could not go to the Loskis' for dinner, but she looked so lovely and happy that I couldn't. I just couldn't. I took a deep breath, wrapped up a pie, and shuffled across the street behind my brothers and parents.

Chet answered the door. Maybe I should've been mad at him, too, for telling the Loskis about my uncle, but I wasn't. I hadn't asked him not to tell, and he certainly wasn't the one making fun of David.

Mrs. Loski came up behind Chet, whisked us in, and fluttered about. And even though she had quite a bit of makeup on, I was surprised to see the blueness of bags beneath her eyes. Then Mrs. Loski and my mother went off with the pies, my brothers vanished down the hall with Lynetta, and my father followed Chet into the living room.

And wasn't that just dandy? That left me alone in the foyer with Bryce.

He said hi to me and I lost it. I spun on him, snapping, "Don't you speak to me! I overheard you and Garrett in the library, and I don't want to talk to you now or ever!"

I started to walk into the living room, but he stopped me. "Juli! Juli, wait!" he whispered. "I'm not the bad guy here! That was Garrett. That was all Garrett!"

I glared at him. "I know what I heard."

"No! No you don't! I...I was feeling bad about, you know, the eggs and what I'd said about your yard. I didn't know anything about your uncle or what kind of situation your family was in, okay? I just wanted to talk to someone about it."

Our eyes locked for a minute, and for the first time the blueness of his didn't freeze up my brain. "I heard you laugh. He made a joke about me being a retard, and you *laughed*."

"Juli, you don't understand. I wanted to punch him! Really, I did! But we were in the library...."

"So instead you laughed."

He shrugged and looked miserable and sheepish. "Yeah."

I left him. Just walked into the living room and left him. If he was making it up, he was quite an actor. If he was telling the truth, then Chet was right—he was a coward. Either way, I didn't want to be anywhere near him.

I stood beside my father and tried to follow his discussion with Chet about something they'd both read in the paper. My father was saying, "But what he's proposing would require a perpetual-motion machine, so it's not possible."

Chet replied, "Maybe in the context of what scientists know now, but do you rule it out completely?"

At that moment I was feeling absolutely no scientific curiosity. But in a desperate attempt to block Bryce Loski from my mind, I asked, "What's a perpetual-motion machine?"

My father and Chet glanced at each other, chuckled, then shrugged, giving me the sense that they'd just agreed to let me into a secret club. My father explained, "It's a machine that runs without any external power source."

"No electricity, no fuel, no water propulsion, nothing." Chet glanced over my shoulder and asked rather absently, "You think that's a doable thing?"

What had distracted him? Was Bryce still in the foyer? Why didn't he just go away?

I forced myself to focus on the conversation. "Do I think that's a doable thing? Well, I don't really know. All machines use energy, right? Even real efficient ones. And that energy has to come from somewhere...."

"What if the machine generated it itself?" Chet asked, but one eye was still on the foyer.

"How could it do that?"

Neither of them answered me. Instead, my father stuck out his hand and said, "Good evening, Rick. Nice of you to have us over."

Mr. Loski pumped my dad's hand and joined our group, making little comments about the weather. When that topic was all dried up, he said, "And wow, that yard of yours has really come along. I told Chet here that we ought to hire him out. He really knows his pickets, doesn't he?"

He was joking. I think. But my father didn't take it that way, and neither did Chet. I was afraid of what might happen next, but then Mrs. Loski tinkled a little dinner bell and called, "Hors d'oeuvres, everybody!"

The hors d'oeuvres were delicious. But when my father whispered that the teeny-tiny black berries on top of the crackers weren't berries at all, but caviar, I stopped midbite. Fish eggs? Repulsive!

Then my father pointed out that I ate chicken eggs all the time, so why get squeamish over fish eggs? He had a point. I hesitantly finished the cracker, and before long I was having another.

Bryce was standing all by himself across the room,

and every time I happened to look his way, he was staring at me.

Finally I completely turned my back on him and said to my father, "So who's trying to invent a perpetual-motion machine, anyway?"

My father laughed. "Mad scientists all over the world."

"Really?"

"Yes. For hundreds of years."

"Well, what do they do? What's one look like?"

It wasn't long before Chet was in on the discussion. And just as I was finally starting to catch on to magnetism, gyroscopic particles, and zero-point energy, I felt someone standing behind me.

It was Bryce.

I could feel my cheeks flush with anger. Couldn't he see I wanted to be left alone? I took a step away from him, but what that did was open up the group and allow him to move forward. Now he was standing in our circle listening to our discussion!

Well! Surely he was not interested in perpetual motion. I barely was myself! So, I reasoned, continuing our discussion would drive him away. I dove back in, and when the conversation started to peter out, I came up with my own ideas on perpetual-motion machines. I was like a perpetual-idea machine, spinning ridiculous suggestions right out of the air.

And still he wouldn't leave. He didn't *say* anything, he just stood there, listening. Then when Mrs. Loski announced that dinner was ready, Bryce held my arm and whispered, "Juli, I'm sorry. I've never been so sorry about anything in my whole life. You're right, I was a jerk, and I'm sorry."

163

I yanked my arm free from his grasp and said, "It seems to me you've been sorry about a whole lot of things lately!" and left him there with his apology hanging wounded in the air.

It didn't take me long to realize that I'd made a mistake. I should have let him say he was sorry and then simply continued to ignore him. But I'd snapped at him in the middle of an apology, which somehow made me the rude one.

I sneaked a peek at him across the table, but he was watching his dad, who was asking my brothers about graduating and their plans for college.

I had, of course, seen Mr. Loski many times, but usually from a distance. Still, it seemed impossible that I'd never noticed his eyes before. They were blue. Brilliant blue. And although Mr. Loski's were set farther back and were hidden somewhat by his eyebrows and cheekbones, there was no mistaking where Bryce had gotten his eyes. His hair was black, too, like Bryce's, and his teeth were white and straight.

Even though Chet had called Bryce the spitting image of his father, I'd never really thought of them as looking alike. But now I saw that they did look alike, though where his dad seemed kind of smug, Bryce seemed...well, right now he seemed angry.

Then from the other side of the table, I heard, "Your sarcasm is not appreciated, Dad."

Mrs. Loski gave a small gasp, and everyone looked at Lynetta. "Well, it's not," she said.

In all the years we've lived across the street from the Loskis, I've said about ten words to Lynetta, and she's said fewer back. To me she's scary. So it wasn't a surprise to see her glaring at her father, but it was uncomfortable. Mrs. Loski was

164

keeping a smile perched on her face, but she was blinking a lot, glancing nervously around the table. I looked from one person to the next, too, wondering if dinner at the Loskis' was always this tense.

Suddenly Lynetta got up and dashed down the hall, but she was back in a flash with a CD in her hand. And when she put it in the player, I recognized one of my brothers' songs blaring through the speakers.

We'd heard this song, "Candle Ice," pouring out of my brothers' bedroom at least a million times, so we were used to it. But I looked over at my mom, worried that she might be embarrassed by the distorting guitars and the gritty lyrics. This was definitely not caviar music.

She seemed a little uncertain, but in a happy way. She was sharing secret smiles with my father, and honestly, I think she even giggled. My dad was looking amused, although he was very reserved about it, and it took me until the end of the song to realize that he was proud. Proud that this noise came from his boys.

That surprised me. Dad has never been real big on any rendition of my brothers' band, although he's never really criticized it either. But then Mr. Loski started grilling Matt and Mike about how they'd afforded to record their own music, and they explained about working and saving and shopping for good deals on equipment, and that's when I realized why my father was proud.

My brothers were feeling pretty good, too, you could tell. And it was no wonder, with the way Lynetta was carrying on about how great "Candle Ice" was. She was positively gushing, which seemed very odd, coming from Lynetta.

JULIANNA

165

As I looked around, it struck me that we were having dinner with a group of strangers. We'd lived across the street for years, but I didn't know these people at all. Lynetta *did* know how to smile. Mr. Loski was clean and smooth on the outside, but there was a distinct whiff of something rotten buried just beneath the surface. And the ever-efficient Mrs. Loski seemed flustered, almost hyper. Was it having *us* over that was making her nervous?

Then there was Bryce—the most disturbing of all because I had to admit that I didn't really know him, either. And based on what I'd discovered lately, I didn't care to know any more. Looking across the table at him, all I got was a strange, detached, neutral feeling. No fireworks, no leftover anger or resurging flutters.

166   Nothing.

After we'd had dessert and it was time to go, I went up to Bryce and told him I was sorry for having been so fierce when we'd first come in. "I should've let you apologize, and really, it was very nice of your family to have us over. I know it was a lot of work and, well, I think my mom had a really good time and that's what matters to me." We were looking right at each other, but it was almost as though he didn't hear me. "Bryce? I said I'm sorry."

He nodded, and then our families were waving good-bye and saying good night.

I walked behind my mother, who was holding hands with my father, and beside my brothers, who were carrying home what was left of our pies. We all wound up in the kitchen, and Matt poured himself a glass of milk and said to Mike, "That Mr. Loski was sniffing us out pretty good tonight, wasn't he?"

JULIANNA

"No kidding. Maybe he thinks we're hot for his daughter."

"Not me, dude! You?"

Mike got himself a glass of milk, too. "That's Skyler's gig. No way I'd go there." He grinned. "But she was really cool tonight. Did she come down on papa bear or what?"

My dad took a paper plate out of the cupboard and cut a slice of pie. "You boys showed a lot of restraint tonight. I don't know if I could've kept my cool that way."

"Aw, he's just, you know... entrenched," Matt said. "Gotta adjust to the perspective and deal from there." Then he added, "Not that I'd want him as *my* dad...."

Mike practically sprayed his milk. "Dude! Can you imagine?" Then Matt gave my dad a slap on the back and said, "No way. I'm sticking with my main man here." My mom grinned from across the kitchen and said, "Me too."

I'd never seen my father cry. And he didn't exactly sit there bawling, but there were definitely tears welling up in his eyes. He blinked them back the best he could and said, "Don't you boys want some pie to go with that milk?"

"Dude," said Matt as he straddled a chair. "I was just thinking that."

"Yeah," Mike added. "I'm starved."

"Get me a plate, too!" I called as Mike dug through the cupboard.

"But we just *ate*," my mother cried.

"Come on, Trina, have some pie. It's delicious."

I went to bed that night feeling very full and very happy. And as I lay there in the dark, I wondered at how much emotion can go into any given day, and thought how nice it was to feel this way at the end of it.

JULIANNA

And as I nestled in and drifted off to sleep, my heart felt wonderfully...free.

✦ ✦ ✦ ✦ ✦

The next morning I still felt good. I went outside and sprinkled the yard, enjoying the splish and patter of water on soil, wondering when, *when*, that first little blade of grass would spring up into the sunshine.

Then I went out back, cleaned the coop, raked the yard, and dug up some of the bigger weeds growing along the edges.

Mrs. Stueby leaned over the side fence as I was shoveling my rakings and weeds into a trash can and said, "How's it going, Julianna? Making neat for a rooster?"

"A rooster?"

168   "Why, certainly. Those hens need some motivation to start laying more!"

It was true. Bonnie and Clydette and the others were only laying about half the eggs that they used to, but a rooster? "I don't think the neighborhood would appreciate my getting a rooster, Mrs. Stueby. Besides, we'd get chicks and I don't think we can handle any more poultry back here."

"Nonsense. You've spoiled these birds, giving them the whole yard. They can share the space. Easily! How else are you going to maintain your business? Soon those birds won't be laying anything a-tall!"

"They won't?"

"Well, very little."

I shook my head, then said, "They were just my chicks that grew into chickens and started laying eggs. I never really thought of it as a business."

"Well, my runnin' a tab has probably contributed to that, and I'm sorry. I'll be sure and get you the whole sum this week, but consider buying yourself a rooster with some of it. I've got a friend down on Newcomb Street who is positively green over my deviled eggs. I gave her my recipe, but she says hers just don't taste the same." She winked at me. "I'm certain she'd pay handsomely for a supply of my secret ingredient if it became available." She turned to go, then said, "By-the-by, Julianna, you have done a mighty fine job on that front yard. Most impressive!"

"Thanks, Mrs. Stueby," I called as she slid open her patio door. "Thanks very much."

I finished scooping up the piles I'd made and thought about what Mrs. Stueby had said. Should I really get a rooster? I'd heard that having one around made chickens lay more, whether they were in contact with each other or not. I could even breed my chickens and get a whole new set of layers. But did I really want to go through all of that again?

Not really. I didn't *want* to be the neighborhood rancher. If my girls quit laying altogether, that would be just fine with me.

I put away the rake and shovel, clucked a kiss on each of the hens, and went inside. It felt good to take charge of my own destiny! I felt strong and right and certain.

Little did I know how a few days back at school would change all of that.

169

Flipped

After the dinner Juli was nice to me at school. Which I hated. Mad was better than nice. Gaga was better than . . . *nice*. It was like I was a stranger to her, and man, it bugged me. Bugged me big-time.

Then the auction happened, and I found myself with even bigger problems.

The auction is this bogus way the Booster Club raises money for the school. They insist it's an honor to be chosen, but bull-stinkin'-loney to that! Bottom line is, twenty guys get shanghaied. They have to come up with fancy picnic lunches and then be humiliated in front of the whole school while girls bid to have lunch with them.

Guess who made this year's top twenty.

You'd think mothers would say, Hey, there's no way you're going to auction my son off to the highest bidder, but no. Instead, they're all flattered that their son's been elected a basket boy.

Yes, my friend, that's what they call you. Over the P.A. you hear stuff like, "There will be an organizational meeting of the newly elected basket boys in the MPR at lunch today. All basket boys must attend."

Pretty soon you've completely lost your name. You

and nineteen other saps are known simply as Basket Boy.

My mom, of course, was into it, coming up with all sorts of stuff to put in my basket so I'd get the highest bid. I tried to explain that I didn't want to be in Mayfield Junior High's Basket Boy Hall of Fame, and that really, what was in the basket didn't matter. It wasn't like girls were bidding on the basket. When you got right down to it, this was a meat market.

"You eat lunch on campus and that's the end of it. It is hardly a meat market, Bryce. It's an honor! Besides, maybe someone really nice will bid on you and you'll make a new friend!"

Mothers can be in such denial.

And then Garrett bends my ear with the news that Shelly Stalls is breaking up with Mitch Michaelson, and that she, Miranda Humes, and Jenny Atkinson are starting some bidding war over me. "Dude!" he tells me. "The two hottest chicks on campus. And I swear to god, man, Shelly's dumped Mitch because of you. I heard it direct from Shagreer, and dude, Shagreer the Ear knows all." He throws me this nasty grin and says, "Me, I'm rooting for Jumbo Jenny. It would serve you right for being such a basket boy."

I told him to shut up, but he was right. With the way my luck was running, I'd probably get stuck with Jumbo Jenny. I could just see it—six feet of beefy babe downing both halves of my lunch and then coming after me. Jenny's the only girl or guy on campus who can dunk a basketball. The whole gym shakes when she lands. And since she's got no, you know . . . female parabolas, the girl could shave her head and make it in the NBA. Seriously. No one would ever suspect.

Her parents give her anything she wants, too. Rumor has it they converted their garage into a full-on basketball court just for her.

Which meant that in the game of the basket boys, I was as good as slam-dunked.

Unless, *unless* Shelly or Miranda was high bidder. But how could I make sure that happened? My brain went into overdrive, constructing a plan, and in the end I decided that there was only one sensible course of action.

Kiss up to both of them.

Halfway through my first day of doing this, I felt like a skunk. Not that I was being gross about it or anything. I was just, you know, friendly. And even though Shelly and Miranda didn't seem to smell a thing, Garrett did.

"Dude!" he says to me on Thursday. "I can see your game, man."

"What are you talking about?"

"Don't deny it, dude. You're working them both." He comes up and whispers in my ear, "Basket boy or not, I'm in awe."

"Shut up, man."

"Seriously! The Ear says they were, like, clawing each other in P.E. today."

I had to know. "What about . . . Jumbo Jenny?"

He shrugs. "Haven't heard. But we'll find out tomorrow, won't we, dude?"

My mother dropped me off at school on Friday with my stupid oversized picnic basket, and since all basket boys have to dress up, I was choking in a tie and feeling completely dweeblike in slacks and dress shoes.

Kids whistled and shouted, "Oooh, baby!" as I headed up the walkway, and then Jumbo Jenny passed me, taking the front steps three at a time. "Wow, Bryce," she said over her shoulder. "You look . . . *delicious.*"

Oh, man! I practically ran to the classroom where all the basket boys were supposed to meet, and the minute I walked in, I felt better. I was surrounded by other dweebs, who seemed genuinely happy to see me. "Hey, Loski"; "Yo, dude"; "Doesn't this suck eggs?"; "Why didn't you take the bus, man?"

Misery loves company.

Then Mrs. McClure, the president of the Boosters, the lady who lassoed us all, hoofs it through the door. "Oh, my!" she says. "You all look so handsome!"

Not one word about our baskets. Not one little sneak peek inside. No, for all she cared, those puppies were empty.

Meat market?

You better believe it!

"Don't be so nervous, boys," Mrs. McClure was saying. "You're going to have a wonderful day!" She pulls out a list of names and starts ordering us into line. We get numbers; our baskets get numbers; we fill out three-by-five cards to her insane specifications; and by the time she's got us all organized and is sure we know what to do and what not to do, we've missed all of first and most of second period. "Okay, gentlemen," she says.

"Leave your baskets where they are and go to...where are we now? Still in second?" She looks at the clock. "Right. Second."

"What about passes?" some sensible basket boy asked.

"Your teachers have a list. But if they say anything, tell them I say your neckties are your passes. I'll meet you back here when everyone's dismissed for the auction. Got it? Don't dawdle!"

We grumbled, Yeah, yeah, and headed to class. And I can tell you this, not one of the twenty of us listened to a word any of our teachers said that morning. How can you listen with a noose around your neck, pinched toes, and a room full of idiots thinking it's open season on basket boys? Whoever started this stupid tradition ought to be crammed into a basket and tossed downstream without a serving spoon.

I was basket boy number nine. Which meant I had to stand there on the stage in the gym while nearly half the guys got auctioned off. Minimum bid, ten bucks. And if nobody bid, the secret was a teacher was assigned to bid on you.

Yes, my friend, the possibilities for mortification were infinite.

Some of the moms showed up and stood off to the side with their camcorders and zoom lenses, fidgeting and waving and basically acting as dweeby as their sons looked. I should know. My mom took an hour off work to be one of them.

Tim Pello was basket boy number five, and his mom actually *bid* on him. No kidding. She jumped up and down, yelling, "Twenty! I'll give you twenty!" Man, that'll brand you for life. Lucky for Tim, Kelly Trott came up with twenty-two fifty and saved his sorry self from ever-lasting torture as a mama's boy—one of the few fates worse than basket boy.

Caleb Hughes was up next, and he fetched the Boosters all of eleven fifty. Then came Chad Ormonde, who I swear was ready to pee his pants when Mrs. McClure made him step forward. She read his card, pinched his cheeks, and raked in fifteen even.

At this point what stood between me and the auction block was Jon Trulock. And I wasn't exactly interested in what he had in his basket or what his hobbies and favorite sports were. I was too busy scanning the crowd for Jumbo Jenny, sweating my pits off.

Mrs. McClure calls into the microphone, "Do I hear ten?" and it took me a minute to tune in to the fact that no one said "Ten!" No one said anything. "Come on, out there! The lunch is delicious. Strawberry tarts, um..." And Mrs. McClure goes back to reading off the three-by-five about Jon Trulock's lunch.

Talk about embarrassing! This was worse than being a mama's boy. Worse than lunch with Jumbo Jenny! How'd he get voted basket boy if nobody wanted to have lunch with him?

Then off to the right of the crowd I hear, "Ten!"

"Ten? Did I hear ten?" Mrs. McClure says with a fluttery smile.

"Twelve!" came a different voice from the same area.

The first voice came back with "Fifteen!" and all of a sudden I recognized whose voice it was.

Juli Baker's.

I searched through the crowd and found her, hand waving in the air, that *look* all over her face.

"Sixteen!" came the other voice.

There was a pause, but then Juli shoots back with "Eighteen!"

"Eighteen!" cries Mrs. McClure, who looks like she's about to collapse from relief. She pauses, then says, "Eighteen going once . . . Eighteen going twice . . . Sold! for eighteen dollars."

To Juli? She was the last person I expected to bid on a lunch. Anybody's lunch.

Jon staggered back into line. And I knew I was supposed to step forward, but I couldn't budge. I felt like I'd been slugged in the stomach. Did Juli *like* Jon? Is that why she'd been so . . . so . . . *nice* lately? Because she didn't care about me anymore? All my life she'd been there, waiting to be avoided, and now it was like I didn't even exist.

"Step up, Bryce. Come on, don't be shy!"

Mike Abenido shoved me a little and said, "Your turn for torture. Get up there!"

It felt like walking the plank. I just stood up front sweating bullets while the Booster queen dissected my lunch and started running through my list of favorites. Before she's even finished, though, Shelly Stalls calls out, "Ten!"

"What's that?" says Mrs. McClure.

"I'll give you ten!"

"Oh," she laughs as she puts down her notes. "Well, I guess I hear ten!"

"Twenty!" calls Miranda Humes from dead center.

"Twenty-five!" It's Shelly again.

I'm looking around for Jumbo Jenny, praying she's gone home sick or something, while Shelly and Miranda go up by fives. "Thirty!"

"Thirty-five!"

"Forty!"

Then I spot her. She's about twenty feet behind Miranda, cleaning her fingernails with her teeth.

"Forty-five!"

"Fifty!"

"Fifty-two."

"Fifty-two?" interrupts the Booster queen. "Well, this has been lively! And from the looks of this basket, well worth the—"

"Sixty!"

"Sixty-two!" calls Shelly.

Miranda scrambles around trying to beg money off her friends as Mrs. McClure calls, "Going once!" But then Jenny stands up and bellows, "A hundred!"

A hundred. There's a collective gasp, and then the entire student body turns and stares at Jenny.

"Well!" laughs Mrs. McClure. "We have a hundred! That is certainly an all-time record. And such a generous donation to the Boosters!"

I wanted to boost *her,* right off the stage. I was doomed. This was something I would never live down.

Then there's this big commotion, and all of a sudden Shelly and Miranda are standing right next to each

177

other calling, "One-twenty-two . . . fifty! We'll give you one-twenty-two fifty!"

"One hundred twenty-two dollars and fifty cents?" I thought the Booster queen was gonna polka. "You're pooling your resources to have lunch with this fine young man?"

"Yeah!" they call, then look over Jenny's way. Everybody looks over Jenny's way.

Jenny just shrugs and goes back to cleaning a nail.

"Well, then! One hundred twenty-two dollars and fifty cents going once . . . One hundred twenty-two dollars and fifty cents going twice . . . *Sold* to those two beautiful young ladies for an all-time record of one hundred twenty-two dollars and fifty cents!"

178

"Dude!" Mike whispered when I got back in line. "Shelly *and* Miranda? How am I supposed to follow that?"

He didn't even come close. He got Terry Norris for sixteen bucks, and the most anyone else got was forty. And when it was over, all the guys told me, "Dude! You are, like, the man. . . . Score!" but I didn't feel like the man. I felt wiped out.

My mom came up and gave me a hug and a kiss like I'd won a gold medal or something, then whispered, "My little baby," and clickity-clicked off in her high heels, back to work.

So I was wiped out, embarrassed, and then practically dragged to the multi-purpose room by Shelly and Miranda.

The Boosters had outfitted the MPR with little tables for two, all decorated in shades of pink and blue and yellow, with balloons and streamers everywhere. I felt like the Easter bunny with my stupid basket boy lunch clutched in both hands while Miranda held on to one arm and Shelly latched on to the other.

They gave us the biggest table and whisked in an extra chair, and when everyone was seated, Mrs. McClure said, "Boys and girls? I don't think I need to remind you that you are excused from class for the rest of the day. Enjoy your lunches, enjoy your friendships. . . . Take your time, relax, and thanks again for supporting your Boosters. We wouldn't be *us* without *you!*"

So there I was, with the two hottest girls on campus, having lunch. I was "the man," the envy of every other guy in school.

Buddy, I was miserable.

I mean, these two girls may be gorgeous, but what was coming out of their mouths about Jumbo Jenny was embarrassingly ugly. Miranda works herself up to, "What was she thinking? Like you would ever want to go out with *her*, right, Bryce?"

Well, yeah. That was right. But it seemed really wrong to say so. "Look, can we talk about something else?"

"Sure. Like what?"

"I don't care. Anything else. You guys going anywhere this summer?"

Miranda shoots off first. "We're taking a cruise to the Mexican Riviera. We're supposed to stop in all these cool ports and shop and stuff." She flutters her eyelids at me and says, "I could bring you something back. . . ."

Shelly scoots her chair in a little and says, "We're

going up to the lake. My dad has a cabin there, and you can get the most outrageous tan. Do you remember what I looked like at the beginning of this year? I was, like, black. I'm going to do that again, only this time I've got a schedule all worked out so that it's even *every*where." She giggles and says, "Don't tell my mom, okay? She would have a ka-nip!"

And this, my friend, is how the Tan Wars began. Miranda told Shelly that she didn't even notice her tan at the beginning of the year and that the place to really roast is on a cruise ship. Shelly told Miranda that anyone with freckles can't really *get* tan and since Miranda had freckles everywhere, the cruise was a guaranteed waste of money. I choked down my third of the lunch and looked around the room, trying to let it all flow past me.

Then I saw Juli. She was two tables away from me, facing my direction. Only she wasn't looking at me. She was looking at Jon, her eyes all sparkly and laughing.

My heart lurched. What was she laughing about? What were they talking about? How could she sit there and look so . . . beautiful?

I felt myself spinning out of control. It was weird. Like I couldn't even steer my own body. I'd always thought Jon was pretty cool, but right then I wanted to go over and throw him across the room.

Shelly grabbed my arm and said, "Bryce, are you all right? You look . . . I don't know . . . possessed or something."

"What? Oh." I tried taking a deep breath.

"What are you staring at?" Miranda asked. They both

looked over their shoulders, then shrugged and went back to picking at their food.

But I couldn't stop myself from looking again. And in the back of my mind, I could hear my grandfather's voice saying, "The choices you make now will affect you for the rest of your life. Do the right thing. . . ."

Do the right thing. . . .

Do the right thing. . . .

Miranda shook me out of it, asking, "Bryce? Are you in there? I asked, what are *you* going to do this summer?"

"I don't know," I snapped.

"Hey, maybe you can spend some time up at the lake with us!" Shelly said.

It was torture. I wanted to scream, Shut up! Leave me alone! I wanted to run out of the building and keep *on* running until I didn't feel like this anymore.

"Lunch is really delicious, Bryce." Miranda's voice was floating around. "Bryce? Did you hear me? This is really a spectacular lunch."

A simple little thank you would've sufficed. But could I come up with a simple little thank you? No. I turned on her and said, "Can we not talk about food or tans or hair?"

She gave me an uppity little smile. "Well, what *do* you want to talk about, then?"

I blinked at her, then at Shelly. "How about perpetual motion? Know anything about that?"

"Perpetual what?"

Miranda starts laughing.

"What?" I ask her. "What's so funny?"

She looks at me a minute, then snickers. "I didn't realize I'd bid on an intellectual."

"Hey . . . I'm plenty smart!"

"Yeah?" Miranda giggles. "Can you *spell* intellectual?"

"He is too smart, Miranda."

"Oh, stop kissing up, Shelly. You're trying to tell me you're after his *brain*? God, it's making me sick to watch you grovel."

"Grovel? Excuse me?"

"You heard me. He's not going to take you to the grad dance anyway, so just give it up, why don't you?"

And with that, it was all over. One of my mom's flaky apple tarts got ground into Miranda's hair; the extra ranch dressing got smeared into Shelly's. And before Mrs. McClure could say, In the name of Boosters! What are you *doing*? they were rolling on the floor, scratching each other's makeup off.

I took this opportunity to leave my table and head for Juli's. I grabbed her by the hand and said, "I've got to talk to you."

She sort of half-stands and says, "What? What's going on, Bryce? Why are they fighting?"

"Excuse us a minute, would you, Jon?" I pull her away from the table, but there's no place to go. And I've got her hand in mine, and I just can't *think*. So I stop right there in the middle of the room and look at her. At that *face*. I want to touch her cheek and see what it feels like. I want to touch her hair, it looks so incredibly soft.

"Bryce," she whispers. "What's wrong?"

I can barely breathe as I ask her, "Do you like him?"

"Do I . . . you mean Jon?"

"Yes!"

"Well, sure. He's nice and—"

182

"No, do you *like* him?" My heart was pounding through my chest as I took her other hand and waited.

"Well, no. I mean, not like *that*...."

No! She said no! I didn't care where I was, I didn't care who saw. I wanted, just *had* to kiss her. I leaned in, closed my eyes, and then...

She broke away from me.

Suddenly, the room was dead quiet. Miranda and Shelly stared at me through their slimy hair, everyone was looking at me like I'd blown my entire circuit board, and I just stood there, trying to reel in my lips and pull myself back together.

Mrs. McClure took me by the shoulders, guided me to my chair, and told me, "You sit here, and you stay here!" Then she hauled Miranda and Shelly outside, scolding them and telling them to find separate bathrooms and clean up while she ran down the janitor to mop up their mess.

I sat there by myself and didn't even care about covering up. I just wanted to be with her. To talk to her. To hold her hand again.

To kiss her.

Before school was out, I tried to talk to her again, but every time I got close, she'd dodge me. And then when the final bell rang, she disappeared. I looked everywhere for her, but she was just gone.

Garrett, however, wasn't. He tracked me down and said, "Dude! Tell me it isn't true!"

I didn't say a word. I just headed for the bike racks, still hoping to find Juli.

"Oh, man...it *is* true!"

"Leave me alone, Garrett."

"You get hooked up with the two finest chicks on campus, then bail on them for *Juli*?"

"You don't understand."

"You're right, dude. I completely don't understand. Did you seriously try to *kiss* her? I couldn't believe that part. We're talking Julianna Baker? Your nightmare neighbor? The know-it-all nuisance? The coop poop babe?"

I stopped cold and shoved him. Just laid into him with both hands and shoved. "That was a long time ago, man. Knock it off!"

Garrett put both hands up, but moved in at me. "Dude, you have flipped, you know that?"

184   "Just back off, would you?"

He blocked my path. "I can't believe this! Two hours ago you were the man. The man! The whole school was on their knees before you! Now look at you. You're, like, a social *hazard*." He snorted and said, "And, dude, the truth is, if you're gonna be like this, I don't need the association."

I got right in his face and said, "Good! 'Cause you know what? Neither do I!"

I shoved him aside and ran.

≺ ≺ ≺ ≺ ≺

I wound up walking home. In my pinchy shoes, with dirty dishes clanking inside my sticky picnic hamper, this basket boy hiked all the way home. And there was a battle raging inside me. The old Bryce wanted to go back in time, wanted to hang with Garrett and shoot the breeze, wanted to hate Juli Baker again.

Wanted to be the man.

But in my heart I knew the old Bryce was toast. There was no going back. Not to Garrett or Shelly or Miranda or any of the other people who wouldn't understand. Juli *was* different, but after all these years that didn't bother me anymore.

I liked it.

I liked *her*.

And every time I saw her, she seemed more beautiful. She just seemed to glow. I'm not talking like a hundred-watt bulb; she just had this warmth to her. Maybe it came from climbing that tree. Maybe it came from singing to chickens. Maybe it came from whacking at two-by-fours and dreaming about perpetual motion. I don't know. All I know is that compared to her, Shelly and Miranda seemed so ... ordinary.

185

I'd never felt like this before. Ever. And just admitting it to myself instead of hiding from it made me feel strong. Happy. I took off my shoes and socks and stuffed them in the basket. My tie whipped over my shoulder as I ran home barefoot, and I realized that Garrett was right about one thing—I *had* flipped.

Completely.

I trucked down our street and spotted her bike lying on its side on the driveway. She was home!

I rang the bell until I thought it would break.

No answer.

I pounded on her door.

No answer.

I went home and called on the phone, and finally, *finally* her mother answers. "Bryce? No, I'm sorry. She doesn't want to talk." Then she whispers, "Give her a little time, won't you?"

I gave her an hour. Almost. Then I went across the street. "Please, Mrs. Baker. I've got to see her!"

"She's locked herself in her room, dear. Why don't you try phoning tomorrow."

Tomorrow? I couldn't wait until tomorrow! So I went around the side of their house, climbed the fence, and knocked on her window. "Juli! Juli, *please*. I've got to see you."

Her curtains didn't open, but the back door did, and out came Mrs. Baker to shoo me away.

When I got home, my granddad was waiting at the front door. "Bryce, what is going on? You've been running back and forth to the Bakers', climbing over their fence. . . . You're acting like the world's on fire!"

I blurted, "I can't believe this! I just can't believe this! She won't talk to me!"

He led me into the front room, saying, "Who won't talk to you?"

"Juli!"

He hesitated. "Is she . . . mad at you?"

"I don't know!"

"Does she have reason to be mad at you?"

"No! Yes! I mean, I don't know!"

"Well, what happened?"

"I tried to kiss her! In front of this whole room of people, while I was supposed to be having that stupid basket boy lunch with Shelly and Miranda, I tried to kiss her!"

Slowly a smile spread across his face. "You did?"

"I was, like, *possessed*. I couldn't stop myself! But she pulled away and . . ." I looked out the window at the Bakers' house. "And now she won't talk to me!"

Very quietly my grandfather said, "Maybe she thinks this is all a little sudden?"

"But it's not!"

"It's not?"

"No, I mean . . ." I turned to him. "It started with that stupid newspaper article. And I don't know . . . I've been weirded out ever since. She doesn't look the same, she doesn't sound the same, she doesn't even seem like the same person to me!" I stared out the window at the Bakers'. "She's . . . she's just different."

My grandfather stood beside me and looked across the street, too. "No, Bryce," he said softly. "She's the same as she's always been; you're the one who's changed." He clapped his hand on my shoulder and whispered, "And, son, from here on out, you'll never be the same again." 187

≺ ≺ ≺ ≺ ≺

Maybe my grandfather's happy about all this, but I'm miserable. I can't eat; I can't watch TV; I can't seem to do anything.

So I went to bed early, but I can't sleep. I've watched her house from my window for hours now. I've stared at the sky; I've counted sheep. But man, I can't stop kicking myself for what an idiot I've been all these years.

And now how am I going to make her listen to me? I'd scale that monster sycamore if I could. Right to the top. And I'd yell her name across the rooftops for the whole world to hear.

And since you know what a tree-climbing weenie I am, I think it's pretty clear that I'm willing to do anything to get her to talk to me. Man, I'll dive after her into a chicken coop full of poop if that's what it takes. I'll ride my bike all the stinkin' way to school for the rest of eternity if it means being with her.

Something. I've got to come up with *some*thing to show her that I've changed. To prove to her that I understand.

But what? How do I show her that I'm not the guy she thinks I am? How do I erase everything I've done and start over?

Maybe I can't. Maybe it just can not be done. But if I've learned one thing from Juli Baker, it's that I've got to put my whole heart and soul into it and try.

Whatever happens, I know that my grandfather's right about one thing.

I'll never be the same again.

188

The Basket Boys

The Monday after the Loskis' dinner party, Darla tracked me down at school and forced Bryce Loski back into my brain. "Jules! Whoa, girl, wait up! How have you been?"

"I'm fine, Darla, how are you?"

"No, seriously," she whispered. "Are you doing okay?" She shifted her backpack and looked over each shoulder. "I got to thinking, you know, that was just so cold of Bryce. Especially since you've got that soft spot for him."

"Who told you that?"

"Like I haven't got eyes? Come on, girl. It's a given. Which is why I got to worryin' about you. Are you seriously all right?"

"Yes, I am. But thanks for thinking about me." I eyed her and said, "And Darla? It's not a given anymore."

She laughed. "How long's this diet gonna last?"

"It's not a diet. I've just, uh, lost my taste for him."

She looked at me skeptically. "Uh-huh."

"Well, I have. But thanks for, you know, caring."

All through first period I was still feeling strong and right and certain, but then Mrs. Simmons ended the lesson a full fifteen minutes early and said, "Clear your desks of everything but a pen or pencil."

"What?" everyone cried, and believe me—I was right along with them. I was not prepared for a quiz!

"Everything!" she said. "Come on, you're wasting valuable time."

The room filled with grumbles and the sound of shuffling binders, and when we'd all pretty much complied with her request, she picked a stack of bright yellow papers off her desk, fanned them with an evil grin, and said, "It's time to vote for basket boys!"

A wave of relief swept across the room. "Basket boys? You mean it's *not* a quiz?"

She ticked through the stack, counting ballots as she spoke. "It *is* like a quiz in that I don't want you conferring with one another. It's *also* like a quiz in that you have a limited amount of time." She slapped a set of ballots down on the first desk of row one, then went on to the second row. "I will collect them from you *individually* when the bell rings, and I will inspect to see that you have complied with the following instructions." She scooted over to row three. "Choose five, and only five, of the boys on the list. Do *not* put your name on it, and do *not* discuss your choices with your neighbors." She was on to row four now, talking faster and faster. "When you've made your selections, simply turn your sheet over." She slapped the remainder down on the last desk. "Do not, I repeat, do *not* fold your ballot!"

Robbie Castinon raised his hand and blurted out, "Why do guys have to vote. It's lame to have guys vote."

"Robbie...," Mrs. Simmons warned.

190

"Seriously! What are we supposed to do? Vote for our friends or our enemies?"

A lot of people snickered, and Mrs. Simmons scowled, but he had a point. Twenty of the school's eighth-grade boys would be made to pack a picnic lunch for two and be auctioned off to the highest bidder.

"Being a basket boy is an honor—" Mrs. Simmons began, but she was interrupted by Robbie.

"It's a joke!" he said. "It's embarrassing! Who wants to be a *basket* boy?"

All the guys around him muttered, "Not me," but Mrs. Simmons cleared her throat and said, "You *should* want to be one! It's a tradition that has helped support the school since it was founded. There have been generation after generation of basket boys helping make this campus what it is today. It's why we have flower beds. It's why we have shade trees and a grove of apple trees. Visit another junior high sometime and you'll begin to realize what a little oasis our campus really is."

191

"All this from the sweat and blood of basket boys," Robbie grumbled.

Mrs. Simmons sighed. "Robbie, someday when your children go to school here, you'll understand. For now, please just vote for whoever you think will earn a high bid. And class," she added, "we're down to nine minutes."

The room fell quiet. And as I read down the list of over one hundred and fifty eighth-grade boys, I realized that to me, there had only ever been one boy. To me, there had only been Bryce.

I didn't let myself get sentimental. I had liked him for all the wrong reasons, and I certainly wasn't going to vote for him now. But I didn't know who else to vote for. I looked at Mrs. Simmons, who was eagle-eyeing the class between glances at the clock. What if I didn't choose anybody? What if I just turned it in blank?

She'd give me detention, that's what. So with two minutes left to go, I put dots next to the boys I knew who weren't jerks or clowns, but were just nice. When I was through, there were all of ten names with dots, and of those I circled five: Ryan Noll, Vince Olson, Adrian Iglesias, Ian Lai, and Jon Trulock. They wouldn't make basket boy, but then I wouldn't be bidding, so it didn't really matter. At the bell I handed over my ballot and forgot all about the auction.

Until lunchtime the next day, that is. Darla cut me off on my way to the library and dragged me over to her table instead. "Have you seen the list?" she asked.

"What list?"

"The list of basket boys!" She shoved a scrawled copy of twenty names in front of me and looked around. "Your main dish is on it!"

Five from the top, there it was—Bryce Loski.

I should have expected it, but still, this awful surge of possessiveness shot through me. Who had voted for him? Out of one hundred fifty names he must have gotten a lot of votes! Suddenly I was picturing a swarm of girls waving stacks of cash in the Booster ladies' faces as they begged to have lunch with him.

I threw the list back at Darla and said, "He's not my main dish! As a matter of fact, I didn't even vote for him."

"Oooo, girl! You *are* stickin' to your diet!"

JULIANNA

"It's not a diet, Darla. I'm . . . I'm over him, okay?"

"I'm glad to hear it, 'cause rumor is, that bimbette Shelly is already stakin' her claim on him."

"Shelly? Shelly *Stalls*?" I could feel my cheeks flush.

"That's right." Darla waved her list in the air, calling, "Liz! Macy! Over here! I've got the list!"

Darla's friends fell all over themselves getting to her, then pored over the paper like it was a treasure map. Macy cried, "Chad Ormonde's on it! He is so cute. I'd go ten bucks on him, easy!"

"And Denny's on it, too!" Liz squealed. "That boy is"— she shivered and giggled—"fi-yi-*yine*!"

Macy's top lip curled a little and she said, "Jon Trulock? Jon *Tru*lock? How did he get on this list?"

For a moment I couldn't believe my ears. I snatched the paper out of Macy's hand. "Are you sure?"

"Right there," she said, pointing to his name. "Who do you suppose voted for him?"

"The quiet girls, I guess," Darla said. "Me, I'm more interested in Mike Abenido. Have I got any competition?"

Macy laughed, "If you're in, I'm out!"

"Me too," said Liz.

"How about you, Jules?" Darla asked me. "Bringin' spare change on Friday?"

"No!"

"You get to miss the second half of school. . . ."

"No! I'm not bidding. Not on anyone!"

She laughed. "Good for you."

That afternoon I rode home from school brooding about Bryce and the whole basket boy auction. I could feel myself backsliding about Bryce. But why should I care if Shelly liked him? I shouldn't even be thinking about him!

When I wasn't thinking about Bryce, I was worrying about poor Jon Trulock. He *was* quiet, and I felt sorry for him, having to clutch a basket and be auctioned off in front of the whole student body. What had I done to him?

But as I bounced up our drive, basket boys bounced right out of my mind. Was that green I saw poking out of the dirt? Yes! Yes, it was! I dropped the bike and got down on my hands and knees. They were so thin, so small, so far apart! They barely made a difference in the vastness of the black dirt, and yet there they were. Pushing their way through to the afternoon sun.

I ran in the house, calling, "Mom! Mom, there's grass!"

"Really?" She emerged from the bathroom with her cleaning gloves and a pail. "I was wondering if it was ever going to spring up."

"Well, it has! Come! Come and see!"

She wasn't too impressed at first. But after I made her get down on her hands and knees and really look, she smiled and said, "They're so delicate...."

"They look like they're yawning, don't they?"

She cocked her head a bit and looked a little closer. "Yawning?"

"Well, more stretching, I guess. Like they're sitting up in their little bed of dirt with their arms stretched way high, saying, Good morning, world!"

She laughed and said, "Yes, they do!"

I got up and uncoiled the hose. "I think they need a wake-up shower, don't you?"

194

JULIANNA

My mom agreed and left me to my singing and sprinkling. And I was completely lost in the joy of my little green blades of new life when I heard the school bus rumble to a stop up on Collier Street.

Bryce. His name shot through my brain, and with it came a panic I didn't seem able to control. Before I could stop myself, I dropped the hose and dashed inside.

I locked myself in my room and tried to do my homework. Where was my peace? Where was my resolve? Where was my sanity? Had they left me because Shelly Stalls was after him? Was it just some old rivalry making me feel this way? I had to get past Bryce and Shelly. They deserved each other—let them have each other!

But in my heart I knew that just like the new grass, I wasn't strong enough yet to be walked on. And until I was, there was only one solution: I had to stay away from him. I needed to rope him *out* of my life.

So I closed my ears to the news of basket boys and steered clear of Bryce at school. And when I did happen to run into him, I simply said hello like he was someone I barely even knew.

It was working, too! I was growing stronger by the day. Who cared about auctions and basket boys? I didn't!

Friday morning I got up early, collected what few eggs there were in the coop, watered the front yard, which was by now definitely green, ate breakfast, and got ready for school.

But as I was running a brush through my hair, I couldn't help thinking about Shelly Stalls. It was auction day. She'd probably been up since five, making her hair into some impossibly pouffy do.

195

JULIANNA

So what? I told myself. So what? But as I was throwing on my windbreaker, I eyed my money tin and hesitated. What if...

No! No-no-no!

I ran to the garage, got my bike, and pushed out of the driveway. And I was in the street and on my way when Mrs. Stueby flew right in my path. "Julianna," she called, waving her hand through the air. "Here, dear. Take this. I'm so sorry it's taken me this long to get it to you. I keep missing you in the mornings."

I didn't even know how much she owed me. At that moment I didn't care. All I knew was the top bill in her hand was a ten, and it was striking terror in my heart. "Mrs. Stueby, please. I...I don't want that. You don't have to pay me."

196

"Nonsense, child! Of course I'm going to pay you. Here!" she said, and waved it out for me to take.

"No, really. I...I don't want it."

She wedged it in the pocket of my jeans and said, "What utter nonsense. Now go! Go buy yourself a rooster!" then hurried back up her walkway.

"Mrs. Stueby...Mrs. Stueby?" I called after her. "I don't *want* a rooster...!" but she was gone.

All the way to school Mrs. Stueby's money was burning a hole in my pocket and another in my brain. How much was it?

When I got to school, I parked my bike, then broke down and looked. Ten, fifteen, sixteen, seventeen, eighteen. I folded the bills together and slid them back into my pocket. Was it more than Shelly had?

All through first period I was furious with myself for even thinking it. All through second period I kept my eyes off of

Bryce, but oh! It was so hard! I'd never seen him in a tie and cuff links before!

Then at break I was at my locker when Shelly Stalls appeared out of nowhere. She got right next to me and said, "I hear you're planning to bid on him."

"What?" I took a step back. "Who told you that? I am not!"

"Someone said they saw you with a whole wad of cash this morning. How much do you have?"

"It's...it's none of your business. And I'm not bidding, okay? I...I don't even like him anymore."

She laughed, "Oh, that'll be the day!"

"It's true." I slammed my locker closed. "Go ahead and waste your money on him. I don't care."

I left her there with her mouth open, which felt even better than getting her in a headlock.

That feeling carried me clear through to eleven o'clock, when the entire student body assembled in the gymnasium. I was not going to bid on Bryce Loski. No way!

Then the basket boys came out on the stage. Bryce looked so adorable holding a picnic basket with red-and-white-checked napkins peeking out from either side, and the thought of Shelly Stalls flipping one of those napkins into her lap nearly made the bills in my pocket burst into flames.

Darla came up behind me and whispered, "Rumor is you've got a wad of cash. Is that true?"

"What? No! I mean, yes, but I...I'm not bidding."

"Oooo, girl, look at you. You feelin' all right?"

I wasn't. I felt sick to my stomach and shaky in the knees. "I'm fine," I told her. "Fine."

JULIANNA

She looked from me to the stage and back to me. "You got nothin' to lose but your self-respect."

"Stop it!" I whispered at her fiercely. It felt like I was having a panic attack. I couldn't breathe. I felt light-headed and wobbly—like I wasn't in control of my own body.

Darla said, "Maybe you should sit down."

"I'm fine, Darla, I'm *fine*."

She frowned at me. "I think I'll stick around to make sure."

The Booster Club president, Mrs. McClure, had been fluttering around the basket boys, fixing ties and giving them last-minute instructions, but now suddenly she was slamming her gavel on the podium, calling into the microphone, "If you'll all settle down, we're ready to begin."

I'd never seen six hundred kids quiet down so fast. I guess Mrs. McClure hadn't either, because she smiled and said, "Why, thank you. Thank you very much." Then she said, "And welcome to the fifty-second annual Basket Boy Auction! I know that your teachers have gone over the procedures with you in homeroom, but I've been asked to remind you of a few things: This is a *civilized* proceeding. No whistling, catcalls, or other degrading behavior will be tolerated. If you wish to place a bid, you must raise your hand high. Bidding without raising your hand is prohibited, and should you decide to be a funny guy, you will be caught and detained or suspended. Are we all clear on that? Good." She looked from one side of the gym to the other. "Teachers, I see that you are in position."

Six hundred heads turned slowly from side to side, looking at the blockade of teachers on either side of the gym.

"Man," Darla whispered, "they're not leaving much room for fun, are they?"

198

JULIANNA

Mrs. McClure continued, "Minimum bid is ten dollars, and of course, the sky's the limit, but we don't accept IOUs." She pointed to her right. "Winning bidders should go directly to the table at the north door when I declare the basket to be sold. And as you're aware, winners and their basket boys have the rest of the school day off and are exempt from tonight's homework in all classes." She smiled out at the blockade. "Teachers, we appreciate your support on this.

"All right, then!" She put on her reading glasses and looked at a three-by-five card. "Our first basket has been brought by Jeffrey Bisho." She looked over her glasses at him and said, "Come on up, Jeffrey. Don't be shy!" He inched forward as she continued. "Jeffrey has brought a scrumptious lunch consisting of chicken salad sandwiches, oriental noodles, baby grapes, iced tea, and fortune cookies." She smiled at him over her glasses.

"Sounds delicious, and sounds like fun! Which," she said, looking back at the crowd, "Jeffrey is! He enjoys skateboarding, skiing, and swimming, but ladies, he also enjoys a day in the park and watching Humphrey Bogart movies." She turned to him and grinned. "They are a kick, aren't they?"

Poor Jeff tried to smile, but you could tell—he wanted to die.

"All right, then," said Mrs. McClure as she whipped off her glasses. "Do I hear ten?"

Not only did she hear ten, she heard twelve, fifteen, twenty, and twenty-five, too! "Going...going...gone!" cried Mrs. McClure. "To the young lady in the purple tunic!"

"Who is that?" I asked Darla.

"I think her name's Tiffany," she said. "She's a seventh grader."

JULIANNA

"Really? Wow. I would never have bid last year! And I...I don't remember bids going up that high, either."

Darla eyed me. "Which tells me that maybe you *would* bid this year? How much you got?"

I looked at her and almost dissolved right on the spot. "Darla, I didn't bring money on purpose! My neighbor made me take it on the way to school because she owed it to me for eggs and—"

"For eggs? Oh, like Bryce was talking about in the library?"

"Exactly, and—" I looked at her looking at me and stopped cold.

"How can you even *think* about bidding on that boy?"

"I don't want to! But I've liked him for so long. Darla, I've liked him since I was *seven*. And even though I know he's a coward and a sneak and I should never speak to him again, I'm having trouble focusing on that. Especially since Shelly Stalls is after him. And now I've got this money burning a hole in my pocket!"

"Well, I can understand the bit about Shelly Stalls, but if you know that boy's just a big piece of fluffy cheesecake that you're gonna regret eating, I can help you with your diet." She put out her hand. "Give me the money. I'll hold it for you."

"No!"

"No?"

"I mean...I can handle this. I've got to handle it."

She shook her head. "Oh, girl. I'm hurting for you here."

I looked back at the stage. The auction was happening so fast! They'd be at Bryce in no time. As the bidding continued, the battle in my head got louder and fiercer. What was I going to do?

J U L I A N N A

Then suddenly the gym fell quiet. You could have heard a pin drop. And standing next to Mrs. McClure looking completely mortified was Jon Trulock. Mrs. McClure was scouring the crowd with her eyes, looking very uncomfortable, too.

"What happened?" I whispered to Darla.

"No one's bidding," she whispered back.

"Do I hear ten?" called Mrs. McClure. "Come on, out there! This lunch is delicious. Strawberry tarts, roast beef and Muenster cheese sandwiches..."

"Oh, no!" I whispered to Darla. "I can't believe I did this to him!"

"You? What did *you* do?"

"I voted for him!"

"Well, you couldn't have been the only one...."

"But why isn't anyone bidding on him? He's...he's so nice."

Darla nodded. "Exactly."

That's when I realized what I had to do. My hand shot into the air and I called, "Ten!"

"Ten?" warbled Mrs. McClure. "Did I hear ten?"

I put my hand up higher and said to Darla, "Say twelve."

"What?"

"Say twelve, I'll outbid you."

"No way!"

"Darla! He can't go for ten, c'mon!"

"Twelve!" Darla called, but her hand didn't go up very high.

"Fifteen!" I cried.

"Sixteen!" called Darla, and eyed me with a laugh.

JULIANNA

I whispered, "Darla! I've only got fifteen."

Her eyes got enormous.

I laughed and called, "Eighteen!" then held her arm down and said, "But that really is all I've got."

There was a moment of silence and then, "Eighteen going once! Eighteen going twice...Sold! for eighteen dollars."

Darla laughed and said, "Whoa, girl! What a rush!"

I nodded. "Yes, it was!"

"Well, no dessert for you. Looks like you got cleaned out by something a little more...uh...nutritious." She nodded toward the stage. "You gonna go up to the table like you're supposed to? Or you gonna stick around and see the carnage?"

I almost didn't have a choice. Before Mrs. McClure could say two words about Bryce or his basket, Shelly called, "Ten!" Then from the middle of the gym came "Twenty!" It was Miranda Humes, with her hand *way* in the air. They went back and forth, back and forth, higher and higher, until Shelly called, "Sixty-two!"

"I can't believe it," I whispered to Darla. "Sixty-two dollars! C'mon, Miranda, come *on*."

"I think she's out. Shelly's got it."

"Sixty-two dollars going once!" cried Mrs. McClure, but before she could say, Going twice! a voice from the back of the gym called, "A hundred!"

Everyone gasped and turned around to see who had called the bid. Darla whispered, "It's Jenny."

"*Atkinson?*" I asked.

Darla pointed. "Right over there."

She was easy to spot, standing tall above the others in the

number-seven basketball jersey she almost always wore. "Wow," I whispered, "I had no idea."

"Maybe she'll slam-dunk him for you," Darla said with a grin.

"Who cares?" I giggled. "She slam-dunked Shelly!"

Mrs. McClure was gushing into the microphone about the record-breaking bid when a big commotion broke out over by Miranda. I spotted Shelly's hair, and my first thought was that there was going to be a fight. But instead, Shelly and Miranda turned to face Mrs. McClure and called, "One-twenty-two fifty!"

I choked down a cry. "What?"

"They're teamin' up," Darla whispered.

"Oh, no-no-no!" I looked over Jenny's way. "Come on, Jenny!"

Darla shook her head and said, "She's through," and she was. Bryce went to Shelly and Miranda for one hundred twenty-two dollars and fifty cents.

≺ ≺ ≺ ≺

It was a little strange, meeting up with Jon and walking over to the multi-purpose room for lunch. But he was just so nice, and I think grateful that I'd bid, that by the time we got situated at our table, I wasn't feeling so awkward or silly. It was just lunch.

Things would have been easier if they hadn't seated me in direct view of Bryce and his little harem, but I did my best to ignore them. Jon told me all about this radio-controlled airplane that he and his dad were building from scratch, and how he'd been working on it for nearly three months, and that over the weekend they were finally going to get to try it out. He told me a funny story about soldering the wires wrong and practically starting a fire in their basement, and I asked him about how a radio-controlled airplane works because I didn't really understand it.

So I'd relaxed a lot and was actually having a good time eating lunch with Jon. And I was *so* relieved that I hadn't bid on Bryce. What a fool I would have made of myself! Watching Shelly and Miranda fawning all over him didn't bother me nearly as much as I thought it would. Really, they looked ridiculous.

Jon asked about my family, so I was telling him about my brothers and their band when a huge commotion broke out over at Bryce's table. Suddenly Shelly and Miranda were rolling on the floor like an enormous furball, smearing each other with food.

Out of nowhere Bryce appeared at our table. He grabbed my hand, pulled me a few feet away, and whispered, "Do you like him?"

I was stunned.

He held my other hand and asked again, "Do you like him?"

"You mean Jon?"

"Yes!"

I can't remember *what* I said. He was looking into my eyes, holding my hands tight, and then he began pulling me toward him. My heart was racing and his eyes were closing and his face was coming toward mine.... Right there, in front of all the other basket boys and their dates and the adults, he was going to kiss me.

204

J U L I A N N A

To *kiss* me.

I panicked. I'd been waiting all my life for that kiss, and now?

I yanked free and ran back to my table, and when I sat down Jon whispered, "Did he just try to kiss you?"

I turned my chair away from Bryce and whispered, "Can we please talk about something else? Anything else?"

People were whispering and looking my way, and when Shelly Stalls came back from cleaning up in the washroom, everyone fell quiet. Her hair looked awful. It was sort of oiled to her scalp and still had little chunks of food in it. She glared at me so hard it looked like she was trying to get laser beams to shoot from her eyes.

A couple of adults steered her back to her seat, and then everyone started whispering double-speed. And Bryce didn't even seem to care! He kept trying to come over and talk to me, but either he'd get intercepted by a teacher or I'd dash away from him before he had a chance to say anything.

When the dismissal bell finally rang, I said a quick goodbye to Jon and bolted out the door. I couldn't reach my bike fast enough! I was the first one off campus, and I pedaled home so hard it felt as though my lungs would burst.

Mrs. Stueby was out front watering her flower bed and she tried to say something to me, but I just dropped my bike in the driveway and escaped into the house. I certainly didn't want to talk about roosters!

My mother heard me slamming doors and came to check on me in my room. "Julianna! What's wrong?"

I flipped over on my bed to face her and wailed, "I am so confused! I don't know what to think or feel or do...!"

205

JULIANNA

She sat down beside me on the bed and stroked my hair. "Tell me what happened, sweetheart."

I hesitated, then threw my hands up in the air. "He tried to *kiss* me!"

My mother struggled not to let it show, but underneath her composed expression was a growing smile. She leaned in a little and asked, "Who did?"

"Bryce!"

She hesitated. "But you've always liked him...."

The doorbell rang. And rang again. My mom started to get up, but I grabbed her arm and said, "Don't get that!" The bell rang again, and almost right after that there was a loud knocking at the door. "Mom, please! Don't get it. That's probably him!"

"But sweetheart..."

"I was over him! Completely over him!"

"Since when?"

"Since last Friday. After the dinner. If he had vanished from the face of the earth after our dinner at the Loskis', I wouldn't have cared!"

"Why? Did something happen at the dinner that I don't know about?"

I threw myself back onto my pillow and said, "It's too complicated, Mom! I...I just can't talk about it."

"My," she said after a moment. "Don't you sound like a teenager."

"I'm sorry," I whimpered, because I knew I was hurting her feelings. I sat up and said, "Mom, all those years I liked him? I never really knew him. All I knew was that he had the most beautiful eyes I'd ever seen and that his smile melted my heart like the sun melts butter. But now I know that inside he's a coward and a sneak, so I've got to get over what he's like on the outside!"

My mother leaned back and crossed her arms. "Well," she said. "Isn't this something."

"What do you mean?"

She chewed the side of one cheek, then moved over to chew the other. At last she said, "I shouldn't really discuss it."

"Why not?"

"Because . . . I just shouldn't. Besides, I can tell there are things you don't feel comfortable discussing with *me*. . . ."

We stared at each other a moment, neither of us saying a word. Finally I looked down and whispered, "When Chet and I were fixing up the yard, I told him how we didn't own the house and about Uncle David. He must have told the rest of the family, because the day before the Loskis' dinner party I overheard Bryce and his friend making cracks about Uncle David at school. I was furious, but I didn't want you to know because you'd think they were only inviting us over because they felt *sorry* for us." I looked at her and said, "You just seemed so happy about being invited for dinner." Then I realized something. "And you know, you've seemed happier ever since."

She held my hand and smiled. "I have a lot to be happy about." Then she sighed and said, "And I already knew they knew about Uncle David. It was *fine* that you talked about him. He's not a secret or anything."

I sat up a little. "Wait . . . *how* did you know?"

"Patsy told me."

I blinked at her. "She did? Before the dinner?"

207

"No, no. After." She hesitated, then said, "Patsy's been over several times this week. She's...she's going through a very rough time."

"How come?"

Mom let out a deep breath and said, "I think you're mature enough to keep this inside these four walls, and I'm only telling you because...because I think it's relevant."

I held my breath and waited.

"Patsy and Rick have been having ferocious fights lately."

"Mr. and Mrs. Loski? What about?"

Mom sighed. "About everything, it seems."

"I don't understand."

Very quietly my mother said, "For the first time in her life, Patsy is seeing her husband for what he is. It's twenty years and two children late, but that's what she's doing." She gave me a sad smile. "Patsy seems to be going through the same thing you are."

The phone rang and Mom said, "Let me get that, okay? Your dad said he'd call if he was working overtime, and that's probably him."

While she was gone, I remembered what Chet had said about someone he knew who had never learned to look beneath the surface. Had he been talking about his own daughter? And how could this happen to her after twenty years of marriage?

When my mother came back, I absently asked, "Is Dad working late?"

"That wasn't Dad, sweetheart. It was Bryce."

I sat straight up. "Now he's *calling*? I have lived across the street from him for six years and he's never once called me! Is he doing this because he's jealous?"

"Jealous? Of whom?"

So I gave her the blow-by-blow, beginning with Mrs. Stueby, going clear through Darla, the auction, the furball fight, and ending with Bryce trying to kiss me in front of everybody.

She clapped her hands and positively giggled.

"Mom, it's not funny!"

She tried to straighten up. "I know, sweetheart, I know."

"I don't want to wind up like Mrs. Loski!"

"You don't have to marry the boy, Julianna. Why don't you just listen to what he has to say? He sounded desperate to talk to you."

"What could he possibly have to say? He's already tried to blame Garrett for what he said about Uncle David, and I'm sorry, but I don't buy it. He's lied to me, he hasn't stood up for me...he's...he's nobody that I *want* to like. I just need some time to get over all those years of *having* liked him."

Mom sat there for the longest time, biting her cheek. Then she said, "People do change, you know. Maybe he's had some revelations lately, too. And frankly, any boy who tries to kiss a girl in front of a room full of other kids does not sound like a coward to me." She stroked my hair and whispered, "Maybe there's more to Bryce Loski than you know."

Then she left me alone with my thoughts.

My mother knew I needed time to think, but Bryce wouldn't leave me alone. He kept calling on the phone and knocking on the door. He even snuck around the house and tapped on my window! Every time I turned around, there he was, pestering me.

I wanted to be able to water the yard in peace. I wanted

not to have to avoid him at school or have Darla run block for me. Why didn't he understand that I wasn't interested in what he had to say? What could he *possibly* have to say?

Was it so much to ask just to be left alone?

Then this afternoon I was reading a book in the front room with the curtains drawn, hiding from him as I had all week, when I heard a noise in the yard. I peeked outside and there was Bryce, walking across my grass. Stomping all *over* my grass! And he was carrying a spade! What was he planning to do with that?

I flew off the couch and yanked open the door and ran right into my father. "Stop him!" I cried.

"Calm down, Julianna," he said, and eased me back inside. "I gave him permission."

"Permission! Permission to do what?" I flew back to the window. "He's digging a *hole*."

"That's right. I told him he could."

"But why?"

"I think the boy has a very good idea, that's why."

"But—"

"It's not going to kill your grass, Julianna. Just let him do what he's come to do."

"But what is it? What's he *doing*?"

"Watch. You'll figure it out."

It was torture seeing him dig up my grass. The hole he was making was enormous! How could my father let him do this to my yard?

Bryce knew I was there, too, because he looked at me once and nodded. No smile, no wave, just a nod.

He dragged over some potting soil, pierced the bag with

the spade, and shoveled dirt into the hole. Then he disappeared. And when he came back, he wrestled a big burlapped root ball across the lawn, the branches of a plant rustling back and forth as he moved.

My dad joined me on the couch and peeked out the window, too.

"A tree?" I whispered. "He's planting a tree?"

"I'd help him, but he says he has to do this himself."

"Is it a..." The words stuck in my throat.

I didn't really need to ask, though, and he knew he didn't need to answer. I could tell from the shape of the leaves, from the texture of the trunk. This was a sycamore tree.

I flipped around on the couch and just sat.

A sycamore tree.

Bryce finished planting the tree, watered it, cleaned everything up, and then went home. And I just sat there, not knowing what to do.

I've *been* sitting here for hours now, just staring out the window at the tree. It may be little now, but it'll grow, day by day. And a hundred years from now it'll reach clear over the rooftops. It'll be miles in the air! Already I can tell—it's going to be an amazing, magnificent tree.

And I can't help wondering, a hundred years from now will a kid climb it the way I climbed the one up on Collier Street? Will she see the things I did? Will she feel the way I did?

Will it change her life the way it changed mine?

I also can't stop wondering about Bryce. What *has* he been trying to tell me? What's *he* thinking about?

I know he's home because he looks out his window from time to time. A little while ago he put his hand up and waved.

JULIANNA

And I couldn't help it—I gave a little wave back.

So maybe I should go over there and thank him for the tree. Maybe we could sit on the porch and talk. It just occurred to me that in all the years we've known each other, we've never done that. Never *really* talked.

Maybe my mother's right. Maybe there is more to Bryce Loski than I know.

Maybe it's time to meet him in the proper light.

212